THE BOBBSEY TWINS
AT THE SEASHORE

THE BOBBSEY TWINS BOOKS
By Laura Lee Hope

———

"The eagle!" Flossie called, jumping up and down

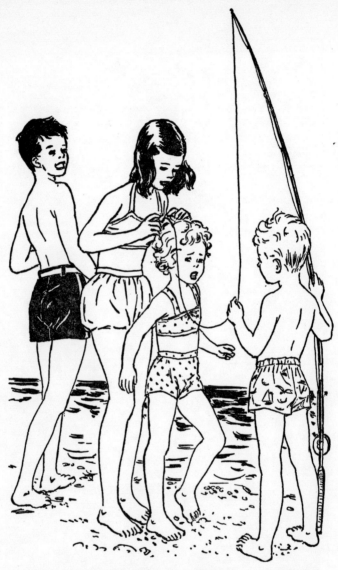

"I'm caught!" Flossie wailed, jumping up and down

The Bobbsey Twins at the Seashore

The Bobbsey Twins
at the Seashore

By

LAURA LEE HOPE

GROSSET & DUNLAP
Publishers   *New York*

The Bobbsey Twins at the Seashore

Preface to the New Edition

You children may not agree, but it seems to me that the biggest difference between children like Freddie and Flossie, and Nan and Bert, and older folk is in their attitude toward the passing of time. It seems to move painfully slowly for you children, but oh, how the years fly past for your fathers and mothers and grandfathers and grandmothers!

I was reminded by my publishers some time ago that it is well over forty years since the first Bobbsey story was written and published. But what brought that fact forcibly to my mind was something that happened a few days ago. I was reading aloud to a little girl who lives next door and who often comes in to visit me and to sample my ginger cookies, just as her grandmother used to come over when I was writing the early Bobbsey books and ask me to read the chapters as they were finished.

We were reading the last chapter of THE

BOBBSEY TWINS—"Merry Days Indoors and Out," as it used to be called. The twins were giving a party and one of Bert's friends was showing magic lantern slides to the enraptured guests.

"What's a magic lantern, Miss Hope?" asked my little neighbor. She never had heard of such a device which we used to think was so marvelous a half-century ago. And why should she? After all, this is the age of television. Magic lanterns belong to the dark ages when people got about by horse and carriage or horse and cutter and there were no such wonders as electric refrigerators or vacuum cleaners. Can you believe it?

I began to see what my publishers had been hinting at—that there is a great deal in the original edition of the book you are about to read that you never saw or perhaps even heard about. So in the new edition I have made a few changes—not in Freddie or Flossie or Nan or Bert, but in some of their surroundings. Before I made them I took up each change with my young neighbor. She gave her approval to each one of them, and I sincerely hope that all of you will feel the same way about it.

LAURA LEE HOPE

CONTENTS

THE BOBBSEY TWINS
AT THE SEASHORE

CHAPTER I

CHASING THE DUCK

"HURRAH, we're off for the seashore!" shouted Bert Bobbsey.

It was a beautiful morning, the very first day of August, that the Bobbseys started for Ocean Cliff. They had spent the month of July at Meadow Brook Farm with Uncle Daniel, Aunt Sarah, and their young cousin Harry.

"Get in, everybody," said Uncle Daniel at the wheel of his station wagon, "or we may miss the train."

"I want to sit in front!" exclaimed little Freddie Bobbsey as he climbed in, " 'cause then I can blow the horn."

The boy beeped the horn three times, which added to the confusion of the Bobbsey family's departure.

"Stop that!" Flossie warned her twin brother,

as she climbed into the very last seat of the car. "You can only blow the horn when Uncle Daniel tells you to."

Soon the station wagon was filled. Mr. Bobbsey sat in front with Bert. Back of them were Mrs. Bobbsey, Aunt Sarah, and Nan, Bert's twin. In the last row were Freddie and Flossie and Cousin Harry. Flossie held Snoop, the kitten, in a basket on her lap.

"All ready?" called Uncle Daniel as he started the motor.

"Wait a minute," Aunt Sarah ordered. "There was another box, I'm sure. Freddie, didn't you fix a shoe box to bring along?"

"Oh, my little duck Downy! He's on the living-room table!" cried Freddie.

"You get him, Bert," Mr. Bobbsey said.

The older boy climbed out and lost no time in bringing the box, which had holes punched in it to give the duck air.

"Now we must get started," said Uncle Daniel, and he started down the driveway.

As you have guessed, there were two sets of twins; Nan and Bert, nearly twelve, dark and handsome, and very devoted to each other, and Freddie and Flossie, almost six, as light as the others were dark, with dimpled cheeks and blonde hair.

The Bobbsey twins lived in Lakeport, where their father owned a lumberyard. Mr. and Mrs. Bobbsey were young themselves and enjoyed good times with their children. The story of "The Bobbsey Twins in the Country" tells about the fun they had and the friends they made at Meadow Brook, the beautiful country home of Uncle Daniel.

Along the road to the station these new friends waved from farmhouses, and called out, "Good-bye! Come again soon!"

Nettie Prentice, whose family was the only poor one in the immediate neighborhood, ran out with a bouquet in her hand. Uncle Daniel pulled up to the side of the road and stopped.

" 'Bye, Nan," the little girl called, handing the flowers to her. "These are for you," she said. "The stems are wrapped in wet cotton. The flowers shouldn't wilt all day."

Nan reached out and took the lovely pink and white and blue bouquet. Nettie's home had an old-fashioned garden, and all kinds of delicate blooms grew near the doorway.

"These are lovely!" Nan exclaimed. "Thank you so much, Nettie."

Nettie said she would miss Nan, for the city girl had always been so kind—even lent her a dress for the wonderful Fourth of July parade.

"I've got the duck you gave me," called Freddie to the little girl, who had given him Downy as a farewell souvenir.

"Give him plenty of water, Freddie, and let him swim a lot." Then Nettie waved again as the station wagon drove off.

They had hardly started again when Freddie cried out, "Mommy, my duck is choking!"

Freddie looked as scared as the duck, which had stuck its head out of one of the holes in the shoe box. The little boy tried to shove the duck back in the box, but could not do it. The yellow bill opened and closed as if Downy were gasping for breath.

"I'll tear the cardboard," said Harry, coming to the rescue. He quickly poked a larger hole around Downy's head and the duck stopped gasping.

There were no more mishaps, and presently they arrived at the station. Uncle Daniel parked near the platform.

"I'll buy the tickets," announced the twins' father, "while you folks get out."

"There's Dinah," called Nan, seeing a plump colored woman near the tracks.

Dinah was the Bobbseys' faithful, good-natured cook, who had ridden down ahead of time on the truck which had brought the baggage. Now she stood guarding it.

"Here comes the train!" cried Freddie excitedly.

Harry, Aunt Sarah, and Uncle Daniel started saying good-bye. Aunt Sarah gave Flossie one more kiss, and Uncle Daniel tossed Freddie into the air and caught him as he came down.

"All aboard!" called the conductor.

"Good-bye!"

"Good-bye!"

"Come and see us at Christmas," called Bert to Harry from the open window of the coach.

"I may see you before that—at the beach," answered Harry, as the wheels began to move.

"We will expect you at Thanksgiving," Mrs. Bobbsey called to Aunt Sarah.

"We'll come if we can," she replied.

"Good-bye! Good-bye!"

"Let's take a last look at good old Meadow Brook," Nan exclaimed, standing up beside her twin.

"Let Snoop see!" shouted Freddie, with his hand on the top of the kitten's basket.

"No, no!" all the Bobbseys called at once. "If you let Snoop out, we'll have the same trouble we had coming up here. Keep him in the basket."

"He wants to look out, too," pouted Freddie. "Snoop liked Meadow Brook, didn't you, Snoopy?" and the little boy put his face close to the basket.

"I'll bet Freddie will have a regular menagerie by the time we get home to Lakeport," Bert ventured with a laugh. "First a kitten, then a duck, and next a—"

"Sea serpent!" exclaimed Freddie, believing that he might find such a monster at the shore. "I promised Uncle Daniel one."

"There goes the last of Meadow Brook," said Nan, as the train rounded a curve and roared over a long bridge. "We had such fun there."

"Isn't it going to be just as much fun at the ocean?" inquired Freddie with some concern.

"Oh, sure," said Bert. "Maybe we will find a sea serpent. Hey, Snoop's getting out!"

Freddie clapped down the lid of the basket, and all the children sat down. Nan and Flossie were side by side, facing Bert and Freddie, who were riding backward. Mr. and Mrs. Bobbsey were right back of the girls. Dinah sat in a seat by herself, with a mountain of boxes and packages alongside her.

On a seat right across the aisle, Nan noticed a little tot sleeping in a bassinet, covered by a white netting. The infant's mother was reading

"What a cute little baby!" exclaimed Nan.

"We must be quiet," said Mrs. Bobbsey, "and let the little baby sleep."

"My duck's a baby, too," Freddie piped up. "It's hot in his box. I think he needs a drink."

With that, Freddie took the top off the shoe box to look at Downy. Instantly there was a flutter. The duck flew out and landed neatly in the aisle.

"Catch him, quick!" cried Bert.

A man near by thought he had him, but the duck dodged, took to the air for an instant, and made straight for a window, which luckily was closed.

"Get him, somebody!" begged Freddie, while other children in the car yelled in delight.

"He's kissing himself," declared one girl, as the frightened little duck perched himself on the window sill and pecked at his reflection in the glass.

"He thinks it's another duck," called Flossie, clapping her hands in glee.

Mr. Bobbsey had gone up cautiously, his soft hat in his hands. Everybody stopped talking and watched.

One more step and Mr. Bobbsey would have the duck under his hat. He raised the hat in his right hand and brought it down.

But Downy was not under it. The baby duck had taken flight just in time.

By this time the twins had joined their father, and frightened little Downy seemed about to surrender. But each time he appeared to be trapped, the duck would flap its little wings and escape again.

The noise had awakened the baby in the bassinet, and her mother took off the netting. This gave Bert an idea.

"May we borrow the netting for a minute?" he asked the baby's mother. "Maybe we can catch our duck with it."

The woman said she would be glad to lend it. Bert crept up on the little duck, who now was perched on a package rack above Bert's head, and raised the net carefully.

CHAPTER II

A MISSING PET

AS BERT was about to fling the net over Downy, the train lurched, pitching the boy forward. He threw his hands up in front of him, sending the net sailing into the air. At the same time the duck hopped off the rack. As he did, the net fell over him as neatly as could be. Duck and net floated to the floor.

"Good pitch, Bert!" Nan said proudly.

Bert got up from the floor of the coach, laughing. "I didn't throw the net on purpose, Nan, but anyway we caught Downy!"

Several children in the car applauded as Bert put the duck back into his box. A couple of boys wanted Freddie to let Downy out again, but Bert overheard the plot and put a stop to it.

But now the other children had found out that the Bobbseys had Snoop with them in a basket, and insisted upon seeing the black kitten.

"We'll hold Snoop tightly," said one of the boys, "and nothing will happen to him."

"But you don't know Snoop," laughed Mrs. Bobbsey. "We nearly lost him on a train a few weeks ago."

"He's the biggest one of my 'magerie," said Freddie, "so we have to take good care of him."

"Menagerie," his mother corrected him.

Mr. Bobbsey, too, insisted that the kitten should not be taken out of the basket, so the boys reluctantly gave in.

At this moment the conductor came to punch the tickets. He asked what was in the basket and in the shoe box. Freddie looked a little frightened but told him.

"Do you have an animal car on the train?" the little boy asked.

The conductor smiled. "No, we don't. Do you like cows and calves?"

"Oh, yes," replied Freddie, "but I didn't like Frisky when she pulled me on a rope."

The conductor asked who Frisky was, and Freddie said she was the nice but naughty calf at Meadow Brook Farm.

"Would you like to see some cows and calves in a car?"

All the twins said "Yes" together.

The conductor said that in a little while they

would stop at a station where there was a loading platform. Here cows and calves would be marched into the cattle cars.

"If your father and mother will let you," said the conductor, "I'll take you off the train and show them to you."

The children could hardly wait for the train to stop. When it did, the conductor took the Bobbsey twins as well as the other children in the car to the platform. They all walked down to the end of the train and crossed the tracks.

"We have only a few minutes," said the conductor, "so stay with me."

On a third track stood a car that had just been loaded. It had slats for sides. Through the openings the children could see cattle crowded closely together. Some were lying on straw.

"Oh, I would never put Frisky in a place like that!" Freddie exclaimed. "She wouldn't have room to move."

"There isn't much room, that's a fact," agreed the conductor. "But you see," he added, grinning, "the cows are not buying tickets!"

One pretty calf tried to push her head between the slats, and Bert managed to give her a couple of crackers from his pocket. She nibbled them eagerly and bobbed her head as if to say, "Thank you!"

"How do they get a drink of water?" asked Flossie, who felt thirsty herself.

"They will be watered tonight," said the conductor, "but hurry now; our train is going to start soon."

The locomotive gave three long whistles and its bell clanged loudly. The children would have liked to wait and watch more cattle cars loaded, but they hurried back inside the train.

When the Bobbseys reached Dinah, her face was pressed close to the windowpane. She heard the twins and turned around.

"I thought sure you'd missed the train," she said. "Did you see a lot of animals?"

"A whole carful," Freddie answered. "Say, Dinah," he went on, looking around perplexed, "where's Snoop?"

"Why— Why—" Dinah looked, too.

The basket was not there!

"Why, where did that go!" Dinah exclaimed.

By this time she was down on her hands and knees, looking under the seat. Bert, Nan, and Freddie, and even Mr. and Mrs. Bobbsey joined in the search, but there was no basket near by.

"Somebody stole my cat!" Freddie wailed. "I just know it!" Tears came to his eyes.

"Now wait," Bert said. "Perhaps one of the boys hid Snoopy somewhere."

"But sure as you live," Dinah said emphatically, "I never left this seat!"

This was true. But Dinah *had* been looking out the window. Mr. and Mrs. Bobbsey were puzzled, too. They admitted having walked to the end of the car to look out when the train was standing still. Someone could have sneaked down the aisle and taken the basket.

"We'd better start hunting," said Nan. "Let's look under every seat. Then we'll look through all the baggage on the racks."

The other passengers in the car were very kind and offered to help the children in their hunt. An old lady said she had seen a boy come into the door at the far end of the car and go out again quickly. But other than this, nobody could give any information about Snoop.

After the children had looked under all the seats, Bert and Nan began to examine the baggage on the racks. Having no luck, they came back to where their parents were sitting.

"He's gone!" Flossie said, brushing aside a tear and putting an arm around Freddie's shoulder. "But don't worry, Freddie, we'll get another cat someday."

"But not like Snoopy," Freddie said, sniffing.

Suddenly Dinah's big eyes lighted up with an idea. "Have you called the kitty?" she asked.

The children had not. They had merely looked for the cat.

"If Snoop's around, he'll answer you," Dinah said. "Come on, I'll help you call him."

Without much hope the children followed Dinah, who began to call the cat. Starting at one door, they worked their way along the aisle to the other end, calling:

"Snoopy, Snoopy, Snoopy cat!"

"Stoop down now and then," Dinah said, " 'cause he may be hiding, you know."

Freddie reached the rear door first.

"I'll just give one more good call," he decided, and did.

"Snoop, Snoop! Come here, Snoop!"

Then above the noise of the train the children heard a faint cry. It sounded like "Meow!"

CHAPTER III

A MILE-LONG SANDWICH

"OH, I heard Snoop!" cried Freddie.

"So did I!" declared Dinah, reaching him.

Instantly the other Bobbsey twins were on the scene. Freddie called out again, and the faint meow came again.

"He's somewhere down here," Bert said, bending over a big suitcase jammed against the last seat in the car.

He pulled out the suitcase, and there behind it was Snoop, safe in his little basket! This time Freddie did take out his pet and cuddle him.

"Oh, poor little Snoop!" he whispered right into the kitten's ear. "I'm so glad to get you back again."

"An' so is Dinah," the cook sighed. "You sure have had a lot o' trouble for one small boy, with two animals to take care of."

The Bobbseys never did find out what mis-

15

chievous person had hidden the basket, but they were glad that the kitten had not been harmed. Snoop had been perfectly safe, but it had been dark and hot where he was hidden. Now he seemed very glad to be out of the basket. He purred contentedly, as Freddie fondled him.

"We had better have our lunch now," suggested Mrs. Bobbsey. "I'm sure the children are hungry."

"Is there a diner on this train?" asked Bert. He had not seen one.

"No need for a diner," chuckled Dinah, getting up and untying one of the boxes alongside her.

The children watched eagerly.

"It's just like a picnic," remarked Flossie, when Dinah handed everybody paper napkins and then served pieces of fried chicken and ham sandwiches.

There were olives and celery, too, besides chocolate cookies and apples and early peaches from Uncle Daniel's farm.

When halfway through a sandwich, Bert asked if he might look at his father's timetable. Then he asked what time it was. Turning back to his brother and sisters, he said:

"Now we're at Rawly. Let's see where we'll be when we finish eating."

Nan giggled. "That'll be fun. How many miles will it take to eat a sandwich?"

Everyone was quiet for a few minutes. Then Dinah spoke up.

"Well, I'm done," chuckled the cook, who was playing the game too. "Bert, how many miles you say it takes me to eat a ham sandwich?"

"Let me see. Five, eight, twelve, fourteen—well, Dinah, I guess you got fifteen miles out of that sandwich."

"Oh, you go 'long!" she protested. "I don't have such a long appetite as that. Fifteen miles!"

Everybody laughed, and the children clapped hands over the length of Dinah's appetite. But when the others had finished, they found that their own appetites were even longer than hers, the average being eighteen miles!

"When will we get to the seashore?" Flossie asked, because she was growing tired of the train ride.

"Not for a while," Mr. Bobbsey answered. "But we're going to get off the train in a little while and go the rest of the way by car."

"Doesn't the train go right to Ocean Cliff any more?" Nan asked.

Her father said it did, but this particular train was a slow one, and he thought they would save time going by car.

"And it's a very pretty ride," added Mrs. Bobbsey. "We might even go past the Fairy Castle. It's somewhere near Ocean Cliff."

"Fairy Castle!" the twins chorused.

Their mother smiled, adding that once upon a time a man had built a playhouse for his children in the form of a castle.

"It's said that one day when the children were playing in it," Mrs. Bobbsey went on, "a lovely fairy appeared and told them where a treasure was hidden."

"And did they find it?" asked Flossie excitedly.

"Yes, they did."

All the children wanted to stop at the castle, and the younger twins said they hoped the fairy would appear while they were there. Now they could hardly wait to get off the train and drive to the spot.

There was one false alarm. The train suddenly slowed down, then stopped. But this was not where the Bobbseys were getting off. The twins were interested, however, in what was happening.

"The train's breaking apart!" cried Freddie.

To be sure, the section beyond the Bobbseys' car suddenly left the rest of the train. Away it went down the track!

But within half a minute another car came rumbling up the track and was hooked on to their train. Mr. Bobbsey explained that certain people were not going to the seashore, so that part of the train was being switched to another track.

"But the new people are going," said Freddie, craning his neck to look into the car which had just been attached.

Nan, too, was looking. Suddenly she said, "Mother, I think I see someone I know. May I go into the car and find out?"

"Why, yes, if you are careful," her mother replied, and Nan started off.

As she left, the train began to move. Bert and his father and mother started reading some magazines they had brought. Freddie and Flossie went to sit with Dinah and hear one of her stories about "When I was a girl and picked cotton down South for my pappy."

Half an hour passed. At the end of that time Nan returned.

"Oh, Mother," she said, "I found Mrs. Manily."

"You mean the director of the Fresh Air Camp at Meadow Brook?" Mrs. Bobbsey asked.

"Yes, Mother. And she says Connie has to go to the seashore. You remember that girl I liked so much? The one who was weak and tired all the time?"

"Yes, I remember her very well. She was a very sweet girl."

"Mother, couldn't we invite her to stay with us awhile at the seashore?" said Nan.

"We are only going on a visit, you know, Nan," her mother replied. "So how could we invite more company? But where is Mrs. Manily? I'd like to talk with her."

Nan led her mother into the next car to see Mrs. Manily. The camp director was very glad to see Mrs. Bobbsey, who had helped the children at the camp with money and clothing.

"Why, how nice to see you again!" said Mrs. Manily. "You are going to the seashore, Nan tells me."

"Yes," replied Mrs. Bobbsey. "We'll be there a few weeks. But what's this Nan tells me about Connie? She's not well yet?"

"No. She will need more rest before she is completely well, and the doctor thinks the seashore air will help her," said Mrs. Manily. "I've just been to our city headquarters to see about transferring her."

"Have you another camp at the shore?" Mrs. Bobbsey asked.

"No. I wish we had," answered Mrs. Manily. "I'm going to Ocean Cliff to see if I can find some place for Connie to stay for a few weeks."

"We're going to visit my sister, Mrs. Minturn, and her husband at Ocean Cliff," said Mrs. Bobbsey. "They have a large cottage and are very kind and hospitable people. If they have no other guests, I think perhaps they would be glad to have Connie stay with them."

"That would be wonderful," said Mrs. Manily. "I was going to do something I have never done before: call on some of the well-to-do people and ask them if they would like to take Connie. We have no extra funds, and I do feel that Connie's is such a deserving case."

"Then you can stop at my sister's first," said Mrs. Bobbsey. "If she cannot accommodate you, she can surely tell you who might. Now won't you join us in our car?"

"I'd like to. Thank you," said Mrs. Manily, getting up.

Nan carried her suitcase into the car where the Bobbseys were sitting.

"Won't it be lovely to have Connie with us!" Nan said to Flossie, telling her the news. "I am sure Aunt Emily will say yes."

"So am I," said little Flossie, whose kind heart

always went out to the less fortunate, just as her Aunt Emily's did. "I know she won't let Connie be sick."

The train was approaching the ocean area now. The view from the car windows had changed. The woodlands and hilly pastures had been left behind. Now through the open windows came the damp, salty tang of the ocean breeze.

"Only half an hour more," said Mr. Bobbsey, looking at his watch.

"Let's have a game of ball," suggested Bert, who never traveled without a ball in his pocket.

The children changed around so that one boy sat in each seat with a girl facing him. They started throwing the ball back and forth.

"The first side with ten misses loses the game," Flossie said, as she threw the ball to Freddie.

He caught it and tossed it to Nan. She threw it to Bert, and the game went along merrily. Suddenly a boy halfway down the car saw what was going on. He called out, "Hey, throw it to me!"

At that moment Freddie had the ball. He pulled back his arm and hurled the ball as hard as he could down the aisle.

But his aim was not good. Instead of going to the boy, the ball went straight toward the face of an old lady who wore glasses. She was reading and did not see the ball coming.

CHAPTER IV

THE FAIRY CASTLE

"LOOK out!" cried Freddie.

But the elderly woman, toward whom the ball was speeding, was so busy reading a book that she did not hear him. The ball hit her on the side of her face, and her eyeglasses flew off.

"Oh, my goodness!" she exclaimed. "My glasses! My glasses!"

"Freddie, you broke the lady's glasses," Flossie said sternly, as everybody in the car looked first at the old lady and then at Freddie, who by this time had slipped very low in his seat.

When Mr. Bobbsey saw what had happened, he hurried over, Nan at his heels.

"Are you hurt?" Mr. Bobbsey asked the old lady.

"No, not hurt," she replied. "But my glasses! I can't see well without them."

"Here they are," Nan said.

Luckily the glasses had fallen into the folds of a coat which was lying on the seat, and had not broken.

"Thank you. Thank you," said the elderly traveler. "I don't know what I'd do without them. They're the only pair I brought with me."

By this time Freddie, at his mother's insistence, had come up to apologize. "I—I'm sorry," he said. "I'll never throw a ball on a train again."

"That's all right, sonny," the woman replied, now smiling. "I have a rambunctious grandson of my own. And 'all's well that ends well.' Isn't that right?"

Freddie said he guessed it was. The kind lady patted his shoulder, and Freddie returned to his own seat. The Bobbseys had hardly settled themselves when a loud voice boomed out:

"Beach Junction! All off for the Junction!"

The conductor repeated his call, looking straight at the Bobbseys, who were to get off here.

"Beach Junction!"

It had been decided that Dinah would continue on the train and look after the larger pieces of baggage, as there would not be room in one automobile for so many people and so much luggage!

"Good-bye, Mrs. Manily! Good-bye, Dinah!" said the twins, and Freddie added, "Beat you to Ocean Cliff!"

"Now wouldn't it be funny," chuckled Dinah, "if old Dinah should get there first? Don't you all go an' have a breakdown!"

"Hurry, children!" said their father.

The Bobbsey family hurried out to the small station, where a number of private cars and taxicabs waited to take passengers to their seashore cottages.

"Sure we haven't forgotten anything we were to bring?" asked Mrs. Bobbsey.

"Bert's got Snoop and I've got Downy," answered Freddie, as if the pets were all that counted.

"And I have my purse and the flowers," answered Nan.

"And I've got my doll," Flossie spoke up.

"I guess we've left nothing important on the train this time," Mr. Bobbsey said with a smile. "And for the first time, too!"

"We've left Dinah," spoke up Freddie. "And she's very 'portant."

The others laughed and agreed that he was right.

Most of the taxis must have been reserved, for

in no time all of them were gone but one, which stood at the rear of the station. An old cabbie nodded at the wheel.

"I'm glad there's one left," said Mr. Bobbsey, and he called to the man.

The dozing driver looked up with a jerk of his head and then called out:

"Hank's super deluxe taxi at your service!"

"Oh, he's joking," Nan said. "There's nothing super about that old cab." And indeed Nan was right, for the old car had outlived its attractiveness many years before.

"Could you take us to Ocean Cliff?" Mr. Bobbsey asked.

"Can't promise," replied Hank, "but you can pile in and we can try it. Which way do you want to go?"

Before the twins' father or mother could answer, Flossie said, "Past the Fairy Castle."

"Sure thing," grinned Hank.

As usual Freddie wanted to sit up front with the driver, so he was put next to Hank, while Flossie sat next to him on her father's lap. The old vehicle roared and chattered over the sandy, rutted roads. It was all the Bobbseys could do to make themselves heard over the noise.

It seemed as if the wheels of the old cab

wanted to stand still, they moved so slowly, and the car creaked and cracked until Hank himself turned around and shouted:

"All right back there?"

"Guess so," answered Mrs. Bobbsey. "When do we come to the castle?"

"Oh, we'll get there," drawled Hank.

"I'm beginning to think we should have gone all the way by train," said Mrs. Bobbsey in alarm, as the motor backfired with a terrific bang.

On they went. Suddenly Hank called out, as they rounded a bend, "There 'tis! The Fairy Castle!"

"Oh!" was all Flossie could say.

Nestled between two little hillsides, with a brook alongside it, stood a miniature castle. It was larger than what Flossie thought fairies needed to live in. Then she remembered it was a playhouse.

Hank's old car could not make the hilly road that led to the castle, so the Bobbseys got out and walked to it. The door was locked, but a key hung beside it and a sign read:

Come in! It may be your luck to see the fairy today. Please lock the door and replace the key when you go.

Flossie and Freddie were holding their breath. Would they see a fairy when the door was opened?

Mr. Bobbsey unlocked it and the small twins, on tiptoe, went into a tiny hall with a tiny grandfather's clock. It was just striking five o'clock.

"Gracious," said Mrs. Bobbsey, seeing the time. "The drive took longer than I thought."

The children were not listening. They had stepped into the living room of the castle. How beautiful it was! And there—standing in front of the fireplace—was the fairy!

Flossie and Freddie were too awed to speak or go closer. Bert, who had not believed the story, was dumfounded. Finally he walked closer. The fairy smiled and put out her hand.

"You're—you're alive!" said Bert hoarsely. Instead of going forward, the boy backed away.

"I am sorry you are afraid," said the fairy in a high, tiny voice. "No treasure ever comes to a child who is afraid."

With this she waved her little wand and a curtain dropped in front of her from the ceiling. Bert was so surprised he did not move for a couple of seconds. Then he sprang forward.

"I'm not afraid!" he said, and pulled the curtain aside.

The fairy had vanished!

Bert was even more astounded. He had been sure a real person had been playing the part. Now he did not know what to think.

Tears rolled down Flossie's cheeks. "You—you scared the fairy away!"

Mr. and Mrs. Bobbsey were puzzled, too. They looked at each other, shaking their heads. Then Mrs. Bobbsey happened to turn around. The fairy was just running through the front hall and up the stairs. She was carrying a mask and a wig in her hand!

Mrs. Bobbsey smiled. "I'm sure the fairy isn't coming back," she said. "Suppose we look around the castle a bit."

The twins walked through the three first-floor rooms, then up the stairs. They admired everything, but all that the younger twins were interested in was seeing the fairy again. Mrs. Bobbsey half expected to see a little dark-haired girl on the second floor, but she remained in hiding.

"Come now!" said Mr. Bobbsey. "If we don't hurry, Dinah will get to Ocean Cliff first."

When the Bobbseys got back to the taxi, Hank had the hood up and was tinkering with the engine. Suddenly smoke puffed out. Hank grinned.

"Got 'er goin'," he said. "I thought for a few minutes you'd have to stay here all night!"

The twins' parents exchanged alarmed looks.

If only another car would come along and pick them up! But no car came, and finally the family climbed in and Hank started off.

"How far is it to Ocean Cliff?" asked Mr. Bobbsey.

Hank shrugged. "I always say that's no way to figure out about gettin' where you're goin'. Just figure on how long it's likely to take you!"

"Well, how long?" said Bert.

"With luck, about an hour."

Everyone groaned. Hank looked hurt. " 'Twasn't my fault you asked to go away from Ocean Cliff."

"What do you mean?" asked Mrs. Bobbsey.

Hank said the road to the Fairy Castle was north, and Ocean Cliff south.

"You mean we have to go all the way back to the station and start out again?" cried Nan.

Hank shook his head. He would take another road, which should be fifteen minutes shorter.

"Anyway, we saw the fairy," said Flossie, and for several minutes the twins talked about the castle.

The old cab groaned and coughed, as if the load were too much for it, but it did go a little faster for nearly half an hour. Then suddenly they hit a bump in the road. Everyone was bounced from his seat. As they settled back, something in the rear of the taxi seemed to come apart. It dragged along the road a few feet, then stopped.

"Sit still," called Mr. Bobbsey to the excited youngsters, as they started to climb out.

Hank got out and walked to the back of the car. Then he returned and said:

"Axle's broken. Well, we're done for now." He announced this with as little concern as if the party had been safely landed on Aunt Emily's porch instead of in the middle of a country road.

"Whew!" said Mr. Bobbsey. "This is a fine mess."

"Sure is. And night comin' on, too," remarked Hank. "Well, I'll go see if I can get some help."

"And what do we do in the meantime? These children can't stay here," Mr. Bobbsey said.

"Well, there's a deserted barn over yonder," Hank answered. "The best thing you can do is to wait in there 'til I fetch somebody to give us a ride."

"How long will that take?" demanded Mr. Bobbsey.

Hank shrugged. "Maybe I'll find a phone. Maybe I'll find a horse and cart."

The Bobbseys watched Hank start off across a field. They waited patiently for fifteen minutes, walking up and down the road.

"Maybe he won't come back at all," fumed Mrs. Bobbsey. "And look at the sky, Richard. It's getting dark. I'm afraid it's going to rain."

"I'm awful hungry," spoke up Freddie.

"Forget it," said Bert, "unless you want to eat grass." He grinned.

"I wish that fairy would come and take care of us," Flossie sighed.

A few drops of rain splashed on their faces. Mr. Bobbsey looked at the roof of the car.

"I'd like to bet this leaks like a sieve," he said. "We'd better go to the barn."

It was hard walking over the uneven ground, and by the time they reached the barn, the rain was starting to come down fast.

"O-o, it's awful dark in here!" said Flossie. The next instant she screamed. "Up there!" she gasped. "What's that?"

CHAPTER V

A BREAKDOWN

HIGH on a rafter two big balls of fire loomed out of the darkness. They looked like two flashlights held close together.

"Oh!" cried Flossie again. "It'll get us!"

A moment later a loud sound came from the same spot. *Whoo-oo-oo!* It grew louder, and the lights blinked.

"It's an owl!" Bert exclaimed.

"I have a few matches," Mr. Bobbsey said, "but we must use them sparingly." He lit one, and the interior of the old barn dimly came into view.

"Look out!" shouted Bert suddenly. "Your head!"

Mr. Bobbsey instinctively ducked, for he thought something was about to hit him. When nothing did, he looked up. Almost directly over his head was an oil lamp, hanging on a nail driven into one of the timbers.

"You've got good eyes, son," Mr. Bobbsey said. "This will save the day—or should I say night!"

Mr. Bobbsey lighted the lantern and gave it to Bert. The boy swung its beam toward the rafter. There sat a large brown-and-white owl, blinking in the light.

"Oh, isn't he pretty!" cried Nan.

"Let's catch him," suggested Bert.

"That's not easily done," said Mr. Bobbsey. "I think we had better not try it now," he advised.

Another fifteen minutes of waiting! Mrs. Bobbsey declared that as soon as the rain stopped, she thought they had better go back to the road and start walking.

In the meantime, at Freddie's suggestion, the twins had begun to play train. Freddie was the engineer and Bert the brakeman, running up and down with the lantern. Nan and Flossie were the passengers.

"Listen!" cried their father suddenly. "I heard a horn!"

Everyone rushed to the open barn door. A horn was blowing, and they could see the headlights of a car.

"Hurrah!" shouted Freddie, and dashed out. The Bobbseys paid no attention to the rain now. They hurried across the field. On the road stood a covered truck.

"I told you I'd get help," Hank called proudly from the driver's seat. "Well, get in, folks. I got all your stuff out o' my car."

"Downy and Snoop?" asked Freddie.

"Yep."

There were no seats in back, so all the children sat on the floor. But the prospect of getting to Ocean Cliff made up for the inconvenience, and when Hank started the motor, all the Bobbseys gave a sigh of relief.

"My," said Nan, putting her arms about Flossie, "I hope nothing more happens."

"I'm glad everything happened," Freddie announced, " 'cause I never saw an owl before, and I never saw a fairy before, and I never rode in a truck like this before!"

The last part of their journey did not take long, and in a short time Hank pulled up in front of the Minturns' cottage. Aunt Emily, Uncle William, and Dorothy rushed to the porch. Dinah followed.

"The Bobbseys! Thank goodness you're here at last! But in this truck!" cried Uncle William in surprise.

"I'm sure glad you're all safe," said Dinah, sighing in relief.

"You got here first like you said, Dinah," grinned Freddie.

While his father paid Hank and took the various small parcels from the truck, the others, all talking at once and hugging one another, told what had happened.

"We were dreadfully worried about you," said Aunt Emily. "We've been waiting for you since three o'clock."

"We found out that the train was late," added Uncle William, "and we waited some more. Then when Dinah told me where you got off, I went to the Junction, thinking you couldn't get a taxi. The station agent said you had left a long while before."

"Honey children, what *did* happen?" demanded Dinah. "Come let me help wash you up while I hear the story."

"We had the awfullest time," Flossie said, as she and Freddie went off with her. "I feel as if we hadn't seen you in a whole year," she sighed.

In the meantime, Nan had given the lovely bouquet to Aunt Emily, and had gone upstairs with her cousin Dorothy.

"Oh, Nan," cried Dorothy, hugging the other girl as tightly as she could, "I thought you never would come!"

"Supper! Supper!" called a voice from the first floor, and the girls hurried down.

"You've had so many things happen today," said Uncle William, "I hope nothing has happened to your appetites."

"I think I could eat two suppers," Bert laughed.

It was a gay party. During the meal Dinah helped the Minturns' maid, being a little jealous that anyone else should look after the wants of "her twins."

"Oh, Dinah," exclaimed Freddie, as she put another glass of milk in front of him, "did you take Snoop out of the basket and did you give Downy some water?"

"I sure did, child," replied Dinah, "and you just ought to see that Downy duck run around the kitchen. Why, he just got one of those fits he had on the train and we had to shut him in the pantry to get hold of him."

"We have a lovely place for him to stay, Freddie," said Dorothy. "There is a little pond out near my donkey barn, and your duck will have a fine time there."

"But he has to swim in the ocean," insisted Freddie, " 'cause we're going to train him to be a circus duck."

"You will have to tie a rope to him, then," Uncle William teased, "because that's the only way a duck can swim safely in the ocean."

"But you don't know about Downy," argued Freddie. "He's wonderful. He even tried to swim on the train without any water!"

"Almost right through the window," Bert said, laughing.

But Freddie took no notice of the way they tried to make fun of the duck, for he felt Downy was really wonderful and would do some amazing things as soon as he had a chance.

When supper was over, Dorothy and Nan went back to Dorothy's room to unpack. As soon as Nan's clothes were neatly put way, the girls sat down on a window seat and looked out at the ocean. The weather had cleared and the moon was shining. It made a brilliant path across the water right to the cottage. Nan looked at it spellbound.

"I think the ocean is so beautiful," she said softly. "It always makes me feel so small and helpless."

"Especially when you are under a big wave," chuckled her cousin, who was full of fun. "I felt that way the other day. Just see my arm."

Dorothy pushed up her short sleeve, displaying a black-and-blue spot.

"How did you get that?" asked Nan sympathetically.

"Ran into a post," returned her cousin with unconcern. "I thought my arm was broken at first. But it's okay now. Come on, we must go downstairs, Nan," she said. "We always sit on the front porch before we go to bed. Mother says the ocean sings a lullaby that makes us all sleep better."

The girls found a caller on the porch. "Oh, good evening, Mrs. Manily," said Nan, and introduced her cousin to the director of the Fresh Air Camp.

The grownups were already talking about Connie, and Mrs. Manily's hunt for a place at the seashore where she might stay.

"Connie's an awfully sweet girl," Nan whispered to Dorothy, "but she's not very strong. The doctor thinks she ought to come down here."

"Why doesn't Connie stay with us?" Dorothy spoke up impulsively.

"Dorothy dear," her mother smiled, "you've taken the words out of my mouth."

"You mean," said Nan excitedly, "that Connie *may* stay here? Oh, Aunt Emily, you're wonderful!" she cried.

CHAPTER VI

DOODLE AND DANDY

NAN WENT to sleep that night particularly happy. Connie was coming for a visit!

It seemed as if she had been asleep no time at all, when she awoke to see the first light of dawn outside her window. The waves were making a soft sh-sh-ing sound as they broke on the sand. Nan crept out of bed and sat down on the low window seat to see the sun rise.

"What a beautiful place!" she thought. "How lucky Dorothy is to be able to see the ocean from her bedroom window!"

Then Nan also realized how lucky she herself was to be at Ocean Cliff. How wonderful it was to have relatives like the Minturns, who always wanted their home to be filled with children and grownups, and even wanted to share their good times with Connie McLaughlin, who was a stranger to them.

"Oh!" Nan cried out the next moment, for somebody had crept up behind her and clapped two hands over Nan's eyes. "Is that you, Dorothy?" she laughed, getting hold of the fingers that covered her face.

"Yes, it is," said Dorothy, releasing her cousin. "Did you think there was a burglar in here?"

As Dorothy dropped down on the cushions of the window seat, Nan smiled at her. Though her cousin was a tomboy and a tease, still she was a beautiful girl. The rosy dawn on her face made her skin pink and gold, and lighted her eyes, which were deep blue like violets.

"You look like a picture I once saw called the Goddess of Morn," said Nan.

Dorothy giggled at the praise. "Nan, did you have a nightmare?" she asked.

"No, indeed," Nan laughed. "I mean every word of it. Oh, Dorothy, look at that sun coming up out of the ocean!"

"If I had my say," Dorothy pursed her lips, "I'd make Mr. Sun wear a mask until respectable people felt like tumbling out of bed." And Dorothy tumbled back into bed. "Come on, get some more sleep."

"I'm sorry I woke you up," said Nan.

"Makes no difference," Dorothy answered. "I'll pay you back."

Nan knew that some trick was in store for her. She must watch her step.

Nan went back to bed. She was sure she could not sleep any more; but two hours later she awoke for the second time that morning. Dorothy stood grinning at her. She was already dressed.

"Get up, Lazybones!" she said.

"How long have you been awake?" Nan asked.

"Long enough to figure out something. And don't ask me what it is. It's a secret."

With that she skipped out of the room. Nan put on beach clothes and hurried downstairs. Her father and Bert were just coming in from a stroll on the sandy beach.

"This is even better than Meadow Brook," Bert told Nan as she took her place at the breakfast table. "I wish Harry could come and visit us here."

"I'm afraid Aunt Emily has quite a full house now," laughed Mrs. Bobbsey.

"Lots more room up near the roof," Dorothy spoke up, "and it's a shame not to use it when there's so much ocean to spare."

The children laughed, because there surely was plenty of ocean for everybody. After breakfast Dorothy said to the twins:

"Come on, I want to show you my donkeys. I call one Doodle and the other Dandy after Yankee Doodle Dandy."

"Why didn't you call one Uncle Sam?" asked Freddie, who had once played the part of Uncle Sam in a Fourth of July parade.

"Are the donkeys twins?" asked Flossie.

"Not real twins, but they look alike."

Dorothy led them to the stable, and opened the door.

"Oh, aren't they cute!" Nan exclaimed as she went up to pat one of the little gray animals.

"How about a ride in the cart?" Dorothy asked. "I'll harness Doodle and Dandy."

"I'll help," Bert offered.

The others watched as their cousin and Bert fastened all the bright buckles and put the straps together, and then hitched the donkeys to the cart.

The cart was one of those pretty little basket affairs, with seats on the sides. When they got in, Dorothy told Bert he could drive, and the boy felt very much excited as he guided the donkeys. They went down the driveway, then along a little narrow road, and soon were on the sand.

"Oh, isn't this fun!" Nan exclaimed.

"Sure is," Bert replied, making the animals trot.

How thrilling to drive so close to the water! Flossie cried out excitedly every time a wave rolled up and touched the wheels of the cart.

"Look at the little crab!" Freddie cried out. "Let's stop and get him."

"We'll have plenty of time to catch crabs," Dorothy said. "There are some big ones, too, and you must be careful they don't bite your finger or your toe.

"Oh, there's Blanche Bowden," she added, as another little cart, pulled by a pony, came along.

"Hello, Dorothy," called Blanche, reining in her pony beside the donkey cart. "You sure have a lot of passengers today."

Blanche was Dorothy's age, but she was a smaller girl, with black hair and dancing eyes. Dorothy introduced Blanche to her cousins. When she came to Freddie, the little boy said:

"Our donkeys can beat your pony!"

"Oh, is that so!" Blanche replied, her eyes sparkling at Freddie's challenge. "Want to race me?"

"No fair," Dorothy said, laughing. "We have a whole load of people."

"But you have two animals," said Blanche. "That makes up for it."

Dorothy glanced at Bert and Nan. "Shall we have a race?" she asked.

The Bobbseys thought it would be a lot of fun.

"All right," Dorothy said to Blanche, as Bert turned the donkey cart around and drew alongside the pony cart. "We'll have a race."

"There must be some rules," Nan spoke up. "How long will the race be?"

Dorothy shaded her eyes with her hands and looked down the beach.

"See that piece of driftwood?" she asked, pointing to an old log that had been washed ashore on the sand about the distance of a city block away. "Let's make that the finish line."

"All right," Blanche agreed. "Whoever passes that first wins the race. But we both have to go in a straight line."

"Who'll fire the starting gun?" Freddie asked. "We have to have a starter."

"You can start us," Dorothy said. "Just say, 'Ready, set, go!' and we'll be off."

When everybody had agreed to the rules, Bert and Blanche held the reins firmly.

Dorothy, Nan, and the twins held fast to the side of their donkey cart, awaiting the word to be off, and then Freddie cried out:

"Ready, set, *go!*"

"Giddap!" shouted Bert and Blanche at the same time, and the donkeys and the pony started to trot across the sand.

"Oh, she's getting ahead of us!" Flossie shouted, as the pony quickly pulled away.

"Come on!" Bert urged the donkeys. "Hurry, Dandy! Faster, Doodle!"

By this time the donkeys seemed to realize they were in a race. Their long ears flattened out as they ran faster and faster.

"We're gaining! We're gaining!" Nan shouted.

Sand from the donkeys' hoofs now was splattering against the front of the cart, some of it getting into the children's faces. But they hardly noticed it.

"We're going to win!" Dorothy shouted, as the donkey cart came up alongside Blanche's.

All at once a little girl who had been standing on the sand ran directly in front of the carts.

"Get out of the way!" Dorothy screamed.

But the little girl, eager to get down to the water's edge, did not seem to hear. To avoid hitting her, Blanche swerved, missing the child by inches. But in doing so, Blanche drove so close to the donkey cart that their wheels were almost touching.

"Look out! Look out!" Nan cried out, as the two carts swayed from side to side.

CHAPTER VII

MISCHIEF

ON WENT the pony and the donkeys. They were really racing now! As the two carts careened wildly along the beach, Nan and the small twins hung on, too frightened to utter a sound.

"Whoa! Whoa!" cried Bert.

"Whoa!" screamed Blanche.

When they passed the driftwood log, one wheel of the donkey cart bumped into it, giving the riders a terrible jolt. Freddie lost his grip and flew over the side of the cart.

"Stop, Bert, stop!" shouted Flossie.

Bert yanked on the reins as hard as he could. When the cart came to a stop, the children jumped out and raced back to see what had happened to Freddie. They found him sitting on the sand, somewhat dazed.

"Freddie, are you hurt?" Nan cried excitedly, kneeling beside him.

"I—I only hurt my pants," Freddie said, as he got up and brushed himself off. Fortunately, he had landed in a big pile of soft sand that once had been somebody's sand castle.

Several children who had been watching the race now came running over, even the little girl who had unwittingly caused the accident. When they realized that Freddie had not been hurt, they were very much relieved.

"Who won the race?" asked a boy.

"We won," Nan said.

"How do you figure that out?" Blanche asked. "We ended the race together."

One of the older boys standing near by laughed and said Dorothy had won by a nose, as they say in grownups' races.

"What do you mean?" asked Blanche.

"I see," Bert grinned, catching on. "Our team has two noses and your pony has only one, so we won by a nose!"

Everyone laughed, including Blanche, and then the two carts were driven off.

Freddie could hardly find words to tell his mother about the adventure, and also how big the ocean was.

"And the water runs right into the sky at the back," Flossie declared.

"It does seem to, at the horizon," her mother agreed.

"Now girls," Aunt Emily said to Nan and Dorothy the following morning, "Mrs. Manily is bringing Connie down today, so suppose you see that her room is in order. I think the third-floor room over your room will be best."

"All right, Mother," answered Dorothy. "We'll make her room look as pretty as a Valentine," she added impishly.

The two girls, with Flossie looking on, soon were busy dusting Connie's room, which had pretty twin beds in it and a bureau on which they put some flowers.

"We certainly want Connie to enjoy herself," said Nan.

"Sure thing," said Dorothy. "I think I'll sleep up here with her, so she won't be lonesome."

"Let me. I know her better," suggested Nan.

"No," her cousin insisted, so Nan said no more.

When the time drew near for the afternoon train to arrive, Dorothy asked her mother if she and Nan might take the donkeys and cart to meet Connie and Mrs. Manily.

"Why, yes, that would be very nice," Mrs. Minturn replied. "I had intended sending the car, but I think Connie would have more fun riding with you."

"And you can take me along, too," said Mr. Bobbsey, who had to go back to Lakeport.

In a few minutes, Bert had the donkeys harnessed and at the door. Nan, her father, and Dorothy drove off. Within half an hour, they were at the station, Mr. Bobbsey had left, and the girls were greeting the visitors.

Connie was a tall, graceful girl, and Dorothy liked her low voice. But she was very pale.

"You were so kind to invite me!" Connie said, as she took her seat in the cart. "This is such a lovely place!" and she nodded toward the ocean, without giving a hint that she had never seen it before.

Even Mrs. Manily, who knew Connie to be a bit shy, was delighted at the way she smiled and talked with Nan and Dorothy.

When they reached the cottage and Connie unpacked her bag, she brought out something for Freddie. It was a little milk truck with real cans, which Freddie could fill up with "milk" and deliver to customers.

"That is to make you think of Meadow Brook," said Connie, when she gave him the little truck.

"Yes, and when there's a fire," answered Freddie, "I can fill the cans with water and dump it on the fire the way they do in Meadow Brook." Freddie planned to become a fireman, and never tired of talking of putting fires out and climbing ladders.

Connie explained that she had been given the truck as a child. She was sorry she had no gifts for the other children.

"Oh, we didn't expect anything," said Nan quickly.

As there was still an hour before supper, she proposed a walk down to the beach. Connie became very serious when they got to the great stretch of white sand near the waves, and the girls noticed tears in her eyes.

"Maybe she's tired," Nan whispered to Dorothy, and they made an excuse to go back to the house.

All along the way Connie was very quiet, and the other girls were disappointed, for they had expected her to enjoy the walk. As soon as they reached home Connie went to her room, and Nan and Dorothy told Mrs. Minturn about the girl's sudden sadness. Mrs. Minturn went up to see if she could do anything for Connie. She found her crying as if her heart would break.

"Oh, I can't help it, Mrs. Minturn!" Connie sobbed. "It was the ocean. Father—he went away on that big, wild sea!" Again she sobbed almost hysterically.

"Tell me about it, dear," said Mrs. Minturn gently, putting her arm around the little girl. "Was your father drowned at sea?"

"Oh, no; that is, we hope he wasn't," said Connie through her tears, "but sometimes we feel he must be dead or he would write to Mother.

"You see," she began the story, and by this time Nan and Dorothy had come up and were listening, "we had such a nice home and Father was always so good. But a friend of his came and asked him to go on a long voyage. The man said they would make lots of money in a very short time.

"First Father said no, but when he talked it over with Mother, they thought it would be best for him to go, so he went."

Connie stopped speaking and tried hard to keep back further tears.

"When did your father leave?" Mrs. Minturn asked.

"Over six months ago," Connie replied, "and he was to be away only three months at the most."

"But your father surely will come back," said Mrs. Minturn kindly. "No news is so often good news. I shouldn't be discouraged—you cannot tell what day your father may return and with a lot of money, too; perhaps even more than he expected."

This made Connie feel better, and she looked at the pictures of her father and mother which she had set on the bureau. She explained that her pretty mother did not look like this now, because she had worried so much.

"I won't feel this way again while I'm here," Connie promised. "It was only because of the ocean. I'm never homesick or blue."

She jumped up, dried her eyes, and looked as if she would never cry again as long as she lived!

"Yes, you must have a good time while you're here," said Mrs. Minturn. "I guess you need fun more than anything else."

That evening Connie was her bright, happy self again, and the three girls chatted merrily about all the good times they would have at the seashore.

They went to the station with Mrs. Manily, who insisted she must leave. Later they played ball with Flossie and the boys.

The children decided to go to bed early, for there was to be a hunt on the beach before breakfast for interesting shells, and a prize to the child collecting the most. As Dorothy and Connie left Nan at her bedroom door, Dorothy said:

"Good night, Nan. Wait till the clock strikes."

"What do you mean?" Nan asked.

"Wait and see."

Two hours after this, when Nan was sound asleep, there suddenly came the buzz of an alarm clock.

"What was that?" she asked herself, waking up. "An alarm clock!"

She listened carefully. It was in her room. But where?

Finally she found it under the mattress and turned it off.

"So that's what Dorothy meant," Nan smiled, as she got under the covers again and went to sleep.

Ten minutes later Nan was awakened again. *Ding—a-ling—a-ling—a-ling!*

Nan put her head under the covers, but she could not shut out the sound. The bell kept on ringing, so she got up and began another search. She had a long hunt, for the clock was in a hatbox in the closet.

Nan got back into bed, but she could not go to sleep. How many more clocks were hidden around, she wondered?

"And Dorothy is sleeping peacefully upstairs," she thought. "Well, she got square with me for waking her up so early yesterday." Nan smiled.

She was just dozing off again, when a deep, loud *bong bong bong* started. Wearily Nan got up. The clock made so much noise that it was not hard to find it behind a box on the window seat.

Before Nan could snap on a light and figure out how to turn off the alarm, the booming had awakened everyone in the house. Mrs. Bobbsey and Mrs. Minturn rushed into Nan's room.

"Well," said Mrs. Minturn, seeing the clock, "I do believe Dorothy has been up to some of her pranks again. This is an old ship's clock, which belongs to our cook, Susan."

At this moment Dorothy poked her head in the door, and asked innocently, "What's all the racket?"

"Now, Dorothy," said Mrs. Minturn, "I know you've played this trick. But enough's enough. Did you hide any more clocks?"

Dorothy only laughed in reply, but when her mother became insistent, the girl brought two more out of hiding and turned off the alarms.

So Nan was not awakened again that night, nor anyone else in the house, and all the children awoke refreshed and ready for the shell hunt.

CHAPTER VIII

A NEAR ACCIDENT

"MAYBE," said Freddie Bobbsey, "if I eat breakfast first, I can find more shells."

Nan laughed. "It seems to me you're always hungry," she said. "Freddie, breakfast isn't ready, and if you don't come, you'll miss the shell hunt."

Since he did not want to be left behind, the little boy trotted along after the other children. As soon as they reached the beach, they began running here and there.

Flossie was the first one to find an unusual shell. It looked like a tiny cornucopia. As she held it to her ear, she cried out:

"It's trying to whistle!"

Dorothy ran over to look at the shell. She said she had never seen one like it.

"I'll bet you'll win the prize for the most unusual," she said.

The other children found a good many shells of various shapes and sizes, but when they compared their collections, there were duplicates in each case. Flossie was the only one who had something really different.

"There goes the bell," announced Dorothy. "Breakfast is ready. Flossie wins!"

"What's my prize?"

"A big fat piece of candy," said Dorothy.

"I couldn't win 'cause I was too hungry," Freddie spoke up.

"And I couldn't win because I didn't get enough sleep last night," giggled Nan.

"And I couldn't win," said Connie, her eyes twinkling, "because I slept too soundly!"

While they were eating breakfast, Dorothy told Bert that a boy named Hal Bingham was coming over to play with him.

"Hal says he knows everything interesting around here to show you."

"Glad of it," said Bert. "You girls are okay, but a boy needs another fellow in a place like this."

"Here comes Hal now," called Dorothy, as a boy came whistling up the path.

He was taller than Bert, but not much older, and he had a very merry twinkle in his black eyes.

After Hal had been introduced, Mrs. Minturn invited him to breakfast, but he said he had just finished his.

"I came to see if Bert would like to go canoeing on the lake," he said.

The lake was at the rear of the cliff on which the Minturn home stood. Bert already had walked down to see it and wished he might paddle a canoe on it sometime.

"I'd sure like to go," Bert said. "One more pancake, and I'll be ready."

As they walked through a meadow to get to the Binghams' boathouse, Bert asked if the lake was deep.

"Deep enough," Hal replied, and added with a grin, "and if you fall out of a canoe, you can get mighty wet!"

The boathouse was made of rough cedar logs, and Hal said he and his father had built it themselves.

"You certainly made a good job of it," said Bert admiringly. "It's all in the design, of course; the nailing together is the easiest part."

"You might think so, but it's hard to drive a nail in round cedar," Hal replied, as he prepared to untie his canoe.

"What a smooth boat!" exclaimed Bert.

The canoe was pale green and the name *Dor-*

othy was painted on each side just above the water line.

"So you call it *Dorothy,*" Bert grinned.

"Yes, Dorothy's more fun than anybody I know," said Hal.

The boys were in the canoe now, and each took a paddle. The water was so calm that they made good time and soon were at the outlet of the lake.

"Here's where we find water lilies," said Hal. "Sometimes I sell 'em."

"Gee, they are pretty," said Bert, as he put one after another into the bottom of the canoe, their stems dripping.

"There's nothing like them," declared Hal. "Some people—hey, stop tipping the canoe!"

Bert had leaned out too far for one of the lilies. He pulled back.

"I'd like to get that big one," said Bert.

"Careful," Hal warned. "This canoe is awful tippy. If you—"

He had not finished speaking when Bert, who was half standing, began to rock the canoe again.

"Hold on!" shouted Hal.

Bert nearly lost his balance. He dropped his paddle and clung to the side a moment, almost upsetting the craft. His right leg splashed into the water.

"Take it easy!" Hal cried.

He shifted his weight to the opposite side of the canoe until Bert was safe. Then he rescued the floating paddle with his own.

"Whew!" exclaimed Bert. "This *is* tippy."

He took off his shoe and wrung the water out of his sock. By this time the canoe had drifted alongside the big lily. Bert reached out and picked it.

The morning passed quickly, for there was much to see around the lake. Wild ducks tried to find out how near they could fly down to the water without touching it, and occasionally one would splash in.

"What large birds there are around the sea!" Bert remarked.

"They have to be big and strong to stand long trips without food," said Hal. "When the waves are rough, they can't find any fish."

"I've seen birds just like these in museums, all colors, and with all kinds of feathers," said Bert. "Do you ever go shooting?"

"Not in the summer," replied Hal. "But sometimes Dad and I take a run down here at Thanksgiving. That's the time for seaside sport. Why, last year we fished with rakes; just raked the fish up in piles—'frosties,' they call them."

"That must be fun," reflected Bert.

"Maybe you could come this year," continued

Hal. "We might make up a party, if you have a Thanksgiving vacation. We could camp out in our house, and get our meals at the hotel."

"That would be swell!" exclaimed Bert. "Maybe Uncle William would come, and my Cousin Harry from Meadow Brook. By the way, we expect him down for a few days."

"Good!" cried Hal. "There's to be a boat carnival next week. I'll bet he'd like that."

When the boys got back to the boathouse, Bert put on his shoe and sock, which were thoroughly dry by this time, and gathered up the pond lilies.

"Wait'll the girls see these," Bert grinned. "Every one of them will want to go canoeing with you."

"Who's that thin girl?" Hal asked. "Cousin of yours?"

"No, just a friend. Her name's Connie McLaughlin. Her father went away on a ship several months ago and hasn't come back."

"That's just like my uncle," Hal said. "He went to bring back a valuable cargo of wood. He had only a small freighter and a few men. Did you say Connie's name is McLaughlin?"

"Yes. She said they called her father Mac."

"Why, that's the name of a man who went with my Uncle George!" declared Hal. "Maybe he's Connie's father!"

CHAPTER IX

FISHERMAN FREDDIE

BERT was very much excited when he heard the news about Connie's father.

"Where's the ship now? When did you last hear from it?" he asked.

"We don't know a thing about it," Hal answered. "My aunt has tried in every way to find out, too."

The boys decided to tell their parents what they had discovered, but not to mention it to Connie. It might make her sad again.

When Bert and Hal reached the dock, they pulled the canoe up on shore, and made their way back to the house.

"Here they come," said Bert as Connie, Nan, and Dorothy raced to meet them.

"Oh!" cried Dorothy, spying the flowers. "I hope you aren't going to sell them all."

"Give me one, please," pleaded Connie.

"They're beautiful, and I've never had one."

Bert handed one to each girl and then announced the rest were for the house.

"We're going for a swim," announced Dorothy. "Want to come along?"

"Sure thing. We'll get our trunks," said Bert.

Soon Nan, Connie, and Flossie appeared with their suits in neat little rubber-lined bags. Then Freddie and Bert joined them, and all set off for the beach with Mrs. Bobbsey.

Dorothy said they had a roomy bathhouse rented for the season, with plenty of hooks to hang things on, besides a mirror to see how one's hair looked after a swim. She kept her suit down there.

It did not take the girls long to get ready. When they came out, each in a pretty bathing suit of a different color, with a cap in a contrasting shade, the little group made a gay spot of color against the white sand.

Flossie wore a white suit, and with her pretty yellow curls looked like a doll. Freddie's trunks were white, too, as he always had things as near like his twin sister's as a boy's clothes could be.

As soon as Mrs. Bobbsey was ready, they all went into the water. The older twins and Dorothy dived under a wave and came up laughing. Hal Bingham joined them in a few minutes.

"Beat you out to the last post," he called.

All four started off to reach the post, which held the end of the life rope. It was hard swimming against the waves, because they were rough and the tide was coming in.

Dorothy won the race. Then the children tried a new game—walking to shore. This was practically impossible, because the waves kept knocking them down and carrying them toward the rope and the posts.

"Look out, Nan!" called Dorothy suddenly, as Nan stood for a moment adjusting her cap.

But the warning came too late. The next instant a wave picked Nan up and tossed her with such force against a post that everybody thought she must be hurt. Mrs. Bobbsey was frightened, and quickly swam toward her daughter.

For a few seconds Nan disappeared. But presently she bobbed up, out of breath. Hal took her by the hand and helped her to shore.

"Are you hurt?" Mrs. Bobbsey cried.

"No. Just got a little bruise on my arm, Mother," Nan replied. She went right back into the water.

All this time Flossie and Freddie had been playing near the water's edge. They had been digging a sand pit and now Freddie was standing waist deep in it.

Both children had their backs to the water. Suddenly an extra large wave rolled in. It did not stop and break where the others had, but kept on and on up the beach, soaking people who were sitting on the sand.

Poor Freddie and Flossie! The wave not only knocked them both over, but flooded the pit. Flossie was able to get up, but her twin was buried in wet sand up to his chest.

"G-get me out!" he spluttered, unable to move.

"Mommy! Mommy!" screamed Flossie.

Mrs. Bobbsey, who had been helping an elderly woman gather up her bag and other belongings that the water had scattered about, turned around. Seeing Freddie in trouble, she hurried over and with Flossie's help pulled her small son out of the sand.

"I'm afraid we didn't pick a good time for bathing," she said. "The waves are too rough."

Concluding that the other children had better come out of the water, she gazed about for them. Nan was swimming in. Bert and Hal were having a water fight a few feet from shore. Dorothy was out near the last post. Mrs. Bobbsey waved to her to come in.

Suddenly the twins' mother realized that Connie was not in sight. She had been hanging onto the rope only a minute before. Now she was gone!

"Connie!" Mrs. Bobbsey cried frantically.

Bert heard her. He, too, had seen Connie only a moment before. Turning around, he spied the girl just disappearing under a wave. Quick as lightning he dived toward Connie, caught hold of her, and tried to help her stand up.

But Connie was too weak to stand. She sagged against Bert, who quickly put his arm around her. By this time Hal was at his side, and together they helped her in to shore.

"I—I just seemed to lose my strength all of a sudden," gasped Connie. "Th-thank you."

Mrs. Bobbsey was worried about the little girl, and insisted that she lie on the sand for a while.

In the meantime the other children decided to walk down to the far end of the beach and watch a man who was fishing from the shore.

"Say, he's pretty good," said Bert admiringly.

The man had deftly swung his pole around to the right and then, with a whizzing sound, had cast the line out into the deep water.

"I'll say he's good," agreed Hal. "That's not as easy as it looks."

"I'd like to try it," said Freddie, walking up to the man. "Is that hard to do, sir?"

The fisherman turned around and smiled.

"Well, sometimes it is," he said. "Do you want to try it?"

"Oh, yes!" cried Freddie.

The other children stood off to one side, laughing at the idea of Freddie swinging the big pole.

The friendly man brought in his line, then showed Freddie how to hold the pole. He stood behind the little Bobbsey boy, and while Freddie held the pole tightly, the man guided Freddie's arms around—whizz!

"Oh! I've got a bite!" yelled Freddie.

At that moment Flossie let out a scream. "I'm caught!" she wailed, jumping up and down.

Nan ran to her side and tried to untangle the hook, which had caught in Flossie's curls.

"Are you hurt, little girl?" asked the fisherman, rushing up to Flossie.

"No, but I'm not a fish," said Flossie. "Freddie isn't very good, is he?"

"Well, he's a little small to handle such a big pole," grinned the man.

They all laughed merrily at Freddie's first attempt at surf casting, glad that the hook had caused no more damage than pulling Flossie's curls.

Nan suggested that they had better do something that they knew how to do, like playing tag.

After a few minutes of this, Dorothy said she wanted to get a towel, and went off to the bath-house. The others sat down to wait for her. She had just returned and was about to sit down too, when she leaped aside, crying:

"Bert! Look out! The crab! It's got you!"

CHAPTER X

THE PEARL

BERT yelled, as they all looked at the crab. It was giant in size and was clinging to Bert's hand.

"Ouch!" he cried, making a face.

He swung his arm as hard as he could. The crab flew into the air and landed a distance away on the sand. Bert surveyed his pinched finger.

Dorothy had started to run across the sand toward the crab.

"Look out!" Bert warned her.

Instead of listening, Dorothy picked up the crab and walked back. She began to stroke its back, and said:

"Poor little crab! Did Bert hurt you?"

The others held their breath. Dorothy laughed.

"What are you afraid of?" she asked. "Why, this is the nicest crab in Ocean Cliff. I keep him in the bathhouse. Here!" she said, and tossed it to Bert.

The boy jumped aside and looked down at the crab. Then he laughed, for the crab was made of rubber!

"All right, Dorothy. I fell for it. But I'll get even. And anytime you want to give away your rubber crab, I'll take it."

By this time everyone knew the crab had not really injured Bert's finger, and they teased him for thinking it had.

"How about wearing rubber gloves when you play on the beach?" teased Nan.

"Aw, quit it!" begged Bert, and the conversation turned to what they would do next.

"It would be fun to hunt for clams and mussels at Rocky Point," suggested Dorothy.

"Let's not go without Connie," said Nan, and the others agreed to postpone the fun.

Next morning Connie said she felt perfectly well and would love to join the others in the hunt. Since it would be an hour's trip to get to the place and back on foot, Aunt Emily thought it would be wise to take the donkey cart. Then if Connie should become tired, she could sit while the others searched among the rocks.

"Anyhow," said Freddie, "we'll need the cart to bring back my sea serpent."

Freddie really expected to capture one, and when Dorothy heard this, she laughed and said she would bring back a whale! Connie hoped she would find something valuable, too. Maybe a buried treasure!

Chatting merrily, the party started off, with Dorothy driving. Nan, Connie, and the small twins rode with her, while Bert and Hal walked. In a little while they came to a long ledge of rocks running out into the water to Rocky Point.

"Let's climb out on this," Hal proposed, pointing. "It's fun to go to the Point this way."

"But the rocks are slippery, so be careful," Dorothy warned. "I'll drive on and meet you there."

Freddie and Flossie went with Dorothy, because the rocks were too steep for them to climb. Their cousin let them take turns driving Doodle and Dandy to make up for the fun the others were having.

"Let's play follow the leader," Bert suggested.

He led the way, and they all climbed from one big rock to another. Every once in a while Bert would stop and do some stunt which the others had to imitate. He especially liked standing on one foot and making a funny face.

Once, as Nan was imitating him, she let out a squeal. "Bert, give me your hand, quick! I'm slipping!"

Bert tried to cross over to where Nan was,

but lost his own footing and slid down. Connie screamed. Nan managed to scramble to safety, and Bert climbed back onto the rocks.

"We'd better go back," said Connie presently.

She did not want anyone to think she was a sissy, but what if one of them should fall off and strike the rocks, or land head first in shallow water?

The others agreed without an argument. The fun, they all thought, was becoming a little too dangerous.

They returned to the sand and hurried on to where Dorothy and the little twins were waiting at Rocky Point. Freddie already had filled a little pail with shells, and Flossie was busy selecting the finest from the collection to take home.

"Oh, here comes old Bill," said Dorothy.

"Who's he?" Freddie asked.

"A clam digger. And he picks up all sorts of things the tide brings in, and makes souvenirs out of them."

"How does he do that?" Flossie wanted to know.

Dorothy said he made lamps from pieces of driftwood, and toys from crates, and necklaces from shells.

When old Bill reached the children, he said, "Morning, young friends. And how be ye?"

"We're fine," they all said, and Hal added, "We're going to do a little digging."

"No finer place for clams and mussels, and crabs—big crabs," the old man told them.

"Maybe you'll find a rubber one," Nan teased Bert.

The older children took off their shoes and socks and began to dig. Each time they spotted an air hole, they would quickly scoop up the wet sand, and were rewarded many times by finding a clam or a mussel.

Connie had wandered off by herself. Suddenly she spied something and picked it up. Running back to the others, she said:

"Here's an oyster."

It was a small one, and had been washed quite clean by the pounding waves.

"Let's open it," said Hal. "Want me to do it, Connie?"

"Yes."

Hal opened it with his knife, and cried out, "Oh, see here! A pearl!"

"Let me look," said Dorothy, taking the little shell in her hand. "Yes, that surely is a pearl. Connie, maybe you did find a treasure! Sometimes these little pearls are valuable."

"Oh, let me see," pleaded Nan. "I've always wanted to see a pearl in an oyster, but I never could find one. How lucky you are, Connie!"

"Maybe it isn't very good," said Connie, hardly believing that anything of value could be picked up so easily.

"Let's ask old Bill," suggested Dorothy. "He'll surely know."

The beachcomber was not far away, picking up pieces of driftwood that had washed ashore. They ran over and showed him the little pellet.

"It's a pearl, sure as you've alive," he said. "And worth some money, too. It would look right purty in a ring, miss. Better get your pa to have one made."

Connie's expression, which had been happy and excited up to this moment, suddenly became sad. She looked out over the ocean and tears came into her eyes. Nan put her arm around the other girl and led her away.

"I'm sorry old Bill mentioned your father," she said. "But don't worry—he'll come back someday. I just know he will."

"Oh, I hope you're right," Connie said softly.

Nan suggested that perhaps Connie could sell the pearl and send the money to her mother. This made the girl feel better, and she started at once hunting for more oysters.

In fact, everybody wanted to dig for oysters now, but it seemed as if the one Connie had found

was the only oyster on shore. This was not sur-
prising, because the oyster beds were out in
deeper water. Yet every time Freddie found a
clam or a mussel, he wanted it opened at once.
But no one had any luck finding a pearl, and
finally they gave up the search.

"Oh, I see a net," called Bert, running toward
a lot of driftwood in which an old fish net was
tangled.

Bert soon disentangled what proved to be a
large piece of seine, which evidently had come
from the fishing grounds a few miles offshore.

"Just what I want for my room at home!" he
declared. "And smell the salt. When I'm in bed,
I can close my eyes and pretend I'm at Ocean
Cliff."

"If Mother will let you take that smelly old
thing home," said Nan.

"It's a good piece," declared Hal, defending
his friend. "Bert was lucky to find it."

Old Bill had come up now, and he agreed the
seine was a very pretty one.

"I declare!" he said. "I've often looked for a
piece of net like that and never could find that
kind."

Bert offered to give it to him, but the old man
shook his head.

"Findin's keepin's," he insisted. "Hang it on

your wall, lad, 'long with your other things." Old Bill chuckled. "When I was a lad your age, I had so many souvenirs in my room, I could hardly find my cot!"

Freddie had been listening, but all the time he had had his eyes on something that was bobbing in the water. Now he started to run down the beach toward it. The others turned around just in time to see a barrel without a top ride in on a wave.

"It's mine! It's mine!" cried Freddie.

He splashed into the water and grabbed the edge of the barrel. The next instant a giant wave knocked him over. He landed head first inside the barrel, which was carried toward the rocks.

"Get him, somebody!" yelled old Bill, running down the beach.

CHAPTER XI

DOWNY ON THE OCEAN

QUICK as a flash, Dorothy, who was nearest the edge of the water, dashed in after Freddie. As the wave receded, the little boy in the barrel was carried into deeper water.

"I'm coming! I'm coming!" yelled Dorothy.

The next instant she grabbed Freddie's kicking feet and yanked him out of the water-filled barrel. She was just in time, for he had held his breath as long as he could.

All the others except Flossie were in the water now. She had covered her eyes with her hands and was sobbing. Hearing Dorothy say, "You're all right now," she dared to look. Then she ran to meet the others as Freddie was carried back on the beach.

"Freddie's always falling in," sighed Flossie, now over her fright.

"Well, I get out again, don't I?" pouted Freddie, not feeling very happy.

Old Bill smiled, then said, "You youngsters better go home and get your soppin' clothes off. There's a right stiff breeze comin' up, and like as not you'll start shiverin' even before you get to the house."

The old beachcomber was right. By the time they reached the Minturn home, every one of them except Flossie was chilled. Mrs. Bobbsey ordered hot baths. By the time they had bathed and dressed, luncheon was ready.

"Well, your wish is coming true, Bert," said his mother, as they were eating dessert.

"My wish?" Bert repeated.

"Your cousin Harry is coming on the afternoon train. And maybe Aunt Sarah."

"Oh, that's swell!" cried Bert. "I hope they'll stay a long time."

Everyone wanted to go to meet them, but Bert was determined to drive the donkeys over and surprise Harry.

"I'll just take Freddie," Bert offered.

Aunt Emily thought this would be all right, and Bert promised not to make Doodle and Dandy run and become overheated.

At four o'clock he went out to harness the team. Freddie was right at Bert's heels, and the two brothers started early for the station.

"I hope they bring some of their big peaches,"

Bert said, thinking of several prize ones that had not been ripe when the Bobbseys had left the country for the shore.

"And I hope Harry brings me one of his rabbits," said Freddie.

Bert grinned, asking if Freddie did not have enough pets to take care of.

"I only have Snoop and Downy," the little boy answered. "Maybe they'd like to play with a rabbit."

A crowd was at the station when the boys got there, so Bert and Freddie had hard work getting a place for their cart near the platform.

"That's the train!" cried Bert. "Now watch out, so that we don't miss Harry in the crowd." He jumped out of the cart to watch the people as they passed along.

"There he is," cried Freddie from the seat, clapping his hands. "Harry! Harry! Aunt Sarah!" he called, until everybody around the station was looking at him and smiling.

"I'm so glad you came," declared Bert to Harry, while Aunt Sarah was hugging Freddie.

"And I'm awfully glad, too," Freddie told them. "We have to show you lots of things, and Connie found a pearl, and—"

"We'll hear all about it as we ride along," Aunt Sarah interrupted. "Where's the car?"

"We're going to ride in this," Bert said, pointing to the cart.

"But we can't all ride in that," Aunt Sarah said, as Bert offered to help her in. "The poor donkeys!"

"Oh, yes, we can," Bert assured her. "These donkeys are very strong, and so is the cart. I'll put your bag right in here," and he shoved the suitcase under one seat.

"We have a basket of peaches somewhere," said Aunt Sarah. "They came in the baggage car."

"And did you bring a rabbit, Harry?" asked Freddie.

"Couldn't carry any more," laughed Harry. "But I'll save you one." Freddie was glad to hear this.

They started off for the shore. Dorothy, Connie, and Nan were waiting in the driveway, and all shouted a welcome to the visitors from Meadow Brook.

"You came just in time," declared Dorothy. "We're going to have a boat carnival here tomorrow."

"Sounds great!" said Harry enthusiastically. "Can we be in it?"

"Sure," Dorothy replied.

Aunt Emily and Mrs. Bobbsey came out now,

and extended such a hearty welcome that there could be no mistaking how pleased they all were to see Harry and Aunt Sarah. As soon as Harry had a chance to change his clothes, Bert and Freddie said they would show him around.

"Come on down to the lake," Bert suggested. "Hal Bingham may have his canoe out. He's a regular fellow, and we have a lot of fun together."

"But I want to show Harry my duck Downy, first," said Freddie. "He's on the little pond. And he's grown so big, he's—he's just like a turkey!"

Harry thought Downy must be a queer duck if he looked that way, but he only laughed and did not question Freddie's description.

"Here, Downy, Downy!" called Freddie, as they came to the pond where the duck always swam around.

There was no duck to be seen. They looked behind some bushes. Downy was not there.

"Where is he?" Freddie asked anxiously.

"Maybe back of some stones," ventured Harry.

He and Bert joined in the search, but no one could find Downy.

"That's strange," Bert reflected. "He always swims here."

"Where does the pond run to?" Harry inquired.

"Into the ocean," answered Bert. "But Downy never goes far away. Say—do you suppose he went to the big lake? Come on, let's go see."

They hurried over to the lake. "There's Hal now," said Bert. "He's in his father's new rowboat. We'll get in and see if we can find the duck. Hi, Hal!"

Seeing his friends, Hal rowed to the shore in the boat that he was trying out for the first time. Bert introduced his cousin, then said:

"Freddie's duck is lost. Have you seen him anywhere?"

"No, I just came out," replied Hal. "But get in and we'll look for him."

All four got into the boat, and Harry sat next to Freddie, while the other boys rowed.

"Oh, I'm afraid someone has stolen Downy," cried Freddie, "and maybe they'll make—make duck soup out of him!"

"No danger," said Hal, laughing. "No one around here would touch your pet duck. They only shoot wild ones."

"We'd better go back to the pond," Bert suggested.

Hal tied his boat to a stake, and the four boys started off. They walked halfway around the pond, but did not find Downy. When they reached the place where the little pond passed through a tunnel under a road, and opened into the ocean, Hal said:

"Maybe Downy went out to see the ocean."

The boys crossed the bridge and made their way through the crowd of bathers down to the waves.

"Oh, oh!" cried Freddie. "I see him!"

Sure enough, there was Downy, like a tiny yellow speck, bobbing up and down on the waves. Obviously, he was having a fine swim, and was not in the least alarmed at the mountains of water that came rolling in.

"Oh, how can we get him?" cried Freddie, nearly running into the water in his excitement.

"I don't know," Hal admitted. "He's pretty far out."

Just then a lifeguard came along. Freddie always insisted that lifeguards must have a very wonderful time, sitting in the sun all day, and always being ready to rescue people. This time there was something extra special to rescue!

"What's the trouble?" the lifeguard asked, seeing Freddie's distress.

"Downy is out there!" cried the little fellow. "He'll be drowned!"

"Oh!" exclaimed the guard, thinking Downy

was some boy who had swum out too far. "I'll get him!"

Before the other boys had a chance to tell the guard that Downy was a duck, the young man was in his boat, and pulling out toward the spot where Freddie had pointed.

"Someone's drowning!" went up the cry.

Hearing it, numbers of men and boys on the beach plunged into the surf, and followed the lifeguard out into the deeper water.

It was useless for Harry, Hal, or Bert to try explaining to anyone about the duck. They just would not believe it! Another guard had come down to the beach now, and was getting an emergency kit ready in case of need.

"Wait till they find out it's only a duck!" whispered Hal to Bert, watching the lifeguard in the boat. He was nearing the speck on the waves. The boys saw him stop rowing.

"He's got him!" shouted the crowd, also seeing the guard lean over the far side of the boat.

"I guess he had to lay him in the bottom of the boat," someone added.

"Maybe he's unconscious!" a woman said.

At this remark Freddie grew frightened all over again. Maybe something *had* happened to Downy!

CHAPTER XII

LOST IN THE WOODS

SINCE the lifeguard in the boat had his back to the crowd as he pulled ashore, even his companion on land had not yet discovered what he had rescued.

The crowd pressed around so closely now that Freddie was pushed back. But he fought his way through to get near the water.

"He's mine!" cried the little fellow. "Let me have him!"

"It must be his brother," whispered a sympathetic woman.

As the lifeguard pulled up on the beach, the people held their breath.

"He's in a bad way!" insisted several, when there was no movement in the bottom of the boat. Then the guard stooped down and brought up —Downy!

"A duck!" yelled several boys in the crowd,

while the other lifeguard laughed heartily over his preparations to restore a duck to consciousness.

"He's mine! He's mine!" insisted Freddie, as the lifeguard fondled the pretty little yellow duck and the crowd cheered.

"Yes, he does belong to my little brother," Bert said, "and Freddie didn't mean to make you think anybody was drowning. It was just a mistake."

"Oh, it's all right," laughed the guard. "Whenever we think someone's in danger, we don't wait for particulars. He's a very pretty duck all the same, and a fine swimmer, and I'm glad I got him for the little fellow, for likely he would have kept on going straight to Europe!"

"We'll have to watch Downy or he'll take that trip again," said Bert later, when they reached home with the enterprising duck. "And next time he might not come back."

"We could build a fence across the part of the pond where it goes into the ocean," suggested Hal. "Then he wouldn't go away."

Bert thought Downy might fly right over the fence.

"I don't think so," said Hal. "Let's try it, anyway. I've lots of material up in our shed."

"That would be a good idea," agreed Harry.

"We can put Downy in the barn until we get the fence built."

Downy was shut up in his box, back of the donkey stall, for the night.

Next morning the boys got to work, and by eleven o'clock had a strong fence set up. It was not easy to make the pickets stay in the sandy soil, and not be washed away, but finally the job was finished.

They let Freddie set him on the water just beyond the new fence. The duck swam directly toward it and stopped.

Freddie waited breathlessly to see if Downy would fly over, but all the duck did was turn around and swim away. The little boy was gleeful.

"He's a good duck, and he's not going to the ocean any more!" Freddie insisted.

The older boys hoped he was right. When they got back to the dock, they all went swimming until the big sea bell on the corner of the Minturn house rang loudly. It could be heard way down the beach.

"What does that mean?" asked Harry.

"Fifteen minutes before lunch," Bert replied. "Come on, we'll have to get dressed."

Hal asked what they were going to do during the afternoon; whatever it was, he wanted to be included. Bert said he would let Harry decide.

"How far back do these woods run?" Harry asked, looking off beyond the shore line.

"I don't know," Hal Bingham answered. "I never felt like going to the end to find out. Too much to do at the beach. But it's said the Indians had a reservation in there once upon a time."

"Then I'll bet there are lots of arrowheads and stone hatchets around," said Harry enthusiastically. "Let's go there this afternoon."

"We can cross the lake in my canoe," said Hal. "Then we will be right at the edge of the woods."

The three boys met at two-thirty. When they started out, Hal paddled around awhile before deciding just where to tie up, because there was no regular trail into the woods.

Finally a spot was selected. Hal tied the canoe to an old tree which had been uprooted and had toppled into the water. The boys set off through the woods, with Hal in the lead.

"Fine big birds around here," remarked Harry, as a pheasant darted among the trees.

"Yes," said Hal. "And there are grouse and deer."

"Any bears?" grinned Bert.

Hal said bears had been reported by some boys, but he doubted the story.

They had been walking for over half an hour

without seeing any sign of a former Indian reservation, when Bert kicked something.

"Hey, fellows, wait!" he called.

Near his foot lay a small, heart-shaped stone. He bent down and picked it up.

"Let's have a look," Harry said, and his cousin handed over the stone. "Say, it's an arrowhead, an Indian arrowhead!"

The boys examined the stone. It was chipped in such a fashion that the point and edges were sharp.

"Just think," Harry said, as Bert put the arrowhead in his pocket, "the Indians hunted on this very spot hundreds of years ago."

Instantly the three boys were on their knees searching through the brown pine needles for more arrowheads.

"Here's another!" declared Harry, picking up a queer dented stone. "It's Indian all right— I know, because Pop has some, but this is the first one I was ever lucky enough to find."

The boys spent a long time at the spot, digging and scuffing up the ground, and finding several more.

"There must have been a regular battle here," said Hal, examining a pointed, leaf-shaped arrowhead.

"What tribe camped here?" Bert asked.

"I don't know," answered Hal. "But I'm going to find out."

The boys were so busy that they did not notice that dusk was coming on. The dense pines and ferns made day seem almost like twilight.

"Say," said Hal suddenly, "it's getting dark! We'd better pick the trail back to our boat, or we may have to be Indians ourselves and camp out here."

But finding their way back soon proved to be impossible. The boys discovered that the trees were much alike, and in the gloom they could not distinguish the path they had made.

"Well, there's where the sun went down, so we must turn our back to that," advised Hal, as they tramped along, vainly trying to find the way home. What at first had seemed to be fun now turned out to be a serious matter, for the boys were really lost.

"Well, I give up!" said Hal at last, sinking to the ground. "I'm sorry I got you fellows into this. Maybe by morning—"

"We can't give up," Bert said firmly. "We've got to get home tonight, or our families will be terribly worried."

"I might climb a tree and see if I can find the lake that way," Hal suggested.

"It's too dark," Bert told him.

"Let's build a fire," Harry proposed. "That will attract attention and someone will come to rescue us."

The other boys agreed this was a good idea, so they set to work gathering dry wood. They laid the sticks in a crisscross pile over some dry leaves, and then each waited for the other to light the fire. Finally Harry said:

"I haven't any matches."

"Neither have I," Bert shrugged.

"Nor I," said Hal. "This is a nice mess!"

"Well, if we're Indians, we'll have to light the sticks with flint and steel," Harry declared, pulling out the steel blade of his pocketknife.

He had just begun to search for a flint stone when Hal said:

"Listen!"

Something was walking in their direction, trampling the underbrush. The step was slow and heavy.

"Do you suppose it's a bear?" cried Bert.

CHAPTER XIII

A STRANGE CABLEGRAM

THE THREE boys could not see what was approaching, so they did not know which way to run.

"We'll stick together and fight him!" Harry declared bravely.

"When I find out where he is, I'm going to run!" said Hal. "Bears can claw you something awful!"

The boys waited, their hearts pounding. Then suddenly Bert saw a large animal among the trees to his left. It had horns.

"It's not a bear!" he yelled. "It's a cow!"

He and the others burst out laughing. Harry walked up to the cow, which was a black-and-white one, and patted its neck.

"I hope you're on your way home," he said to the cow. "We'll follow you."

The cow seemed to understand. She rubbed

her head against Harry's sleeve, and started to walk through the dark woods.

"If we follow her, she'll lead us out, all right," said Harry, and so the three boys started off after the cow.

Just as Harry had said, the animal made her way to a path, and soon an opening in the trees showed a few scattered houses.

"I know where we are!" exclaimed Hal. "We'll have a long hike home, but I don't mind that. It's better than a night in the woods without blankets."

"We must see that this cow gets home first," said Bert.

There was no need to worry, because at the first farmhouse they came to, a woman met them.

"Oh, you've found Daisy!" she began. "My husband was just going to start out after her. Come, Daisy, you're hungry," and she patted the cow affectionately. "Well, boys, I'm obliged to you. If you will accept some milk, I'll give you each a quart."

"We would be very glad to have some milk," spoke up Bert promptly, "but we didn't bring Daisy here. She brought *us,*" and he told the story.

"I always said Daisy was smart," said the farmer's wife. "Well, you must be hungry. I'll give you each a glass of milk, and some bottles to take home. Growing boys can always drink extra milk. Where do you live?"

"At Ocean Cliff," said Bert.

"Well, I do declare!" laughed the woman, getting the glasses of milk, and taking three bottles from the refrigerator in her kitchen. "Our man goes right by your house tomorrow morning, and if you leave the bottles outside, he will get them. Maybe your mothers might like some rich milk, or buttermilk, or fresh eggs, or freshly churned butter?" she asked.

"Shouldn't wonder," said Bert. "My aunt has lots of company. I'll tell her."

"And if you ever want a drink of milk, and are out this way," the farmer's wife went on, "just knock at my door and I'll see you don't go away thirsty."

After more thanks on both sides, the boys started homeward, each with a bottle under his arm.

"It didn't seem right to take all this milk," remarked Bert, as the boys made their way in the dark along the road to the ocean.

"But we would have offended the lady if we had refused," said Harry. "Besides, we may be able to get her some customers."

"I suppose our folks think we're lost," commented Hal.

"Then they think right," laughed Bert, "at least until fifteen minutes ago."

As they reached a bridge that led to Ocean Cliff, the boys could hear voices down the road.

"That's my father," declared Hal.

"And that's Uncle William," said Bert.

The boys shouted, and the older voices called back in reply. How relieved they sounded!

Presently Uncle William and Mr. Bingham came up, and were so glad to find that Hal, Harry, and Bert safe that they scarcely required any explanation for the delay in getting home. Both men well remembered how easy it is to get lost in the woods, so beyond a word of caution, and a reminder to get the canoe next day, there was not a scolding word spoken.

A little farther down the road, Dorothy, Nan and Connie met the wanderers, and at the Minturn house were three excited mothers, who hugged their boys tightly.

Even Dinah came outside and said she was glad to see them back safe. She did not complain about serving a late dinner to Bert and Harry, and said she had never seen such creamy milk as they had brought from the farmhouse.

"We might take some extra milk from that farm," said Aunt Emily.

So, as Harry had said, the adventure brought good results, for on the following morning, when the man called for the empty bottles, Aunt Emily ordered two quarts a day from him, besides some fresh eggs and butter to be delivered twice a week.

There had been so much excitement about the boys that no one had noticed until now how quiet Connie had been the evening before, and she had scarcely touched her breakfast.

"Connie, aren't you feeling well?" Mrs. Bobbsey asked kindly.

The girl smiled a little. "I'm just not hungry," she answered.

The twins' mother looked at her, took Connie's hands in her own, and said, "Was it something in the letter you received yesterday?"

Connie nodded. She said the letter was from her mother. Mrs. McLaughlin had received a call from a woman also named Mrs. William McLaughlin.

A cablegram had been delivered to her by mistake, saying the *Sea Hawk* had finished loading lumber and was starting home. Both the cable office and the woman had tried to find the right Mrs. McLaughlin, but had not done so until a few days before.

"That's funny," said Dorothy. "Your father knows where you live, doesn't he?"

"Yes," Connie answered, "but the cable was marked *Island City* instead of *Iron City,* where we live."

"Well, the letter should make you very happy," said Mrs. Minturn. "Your father should be home soon."

A tear rolled down Connie's face. "That cable was sent four months ago!" she said. "It took all this time to find us. Father should have been home long before this. Now I'm sure he's lost!"

It was hard for the others to know how to comfort Connie. But Mrs. Bobbsey spoke up, saying she and Mr. Bobbsey had a friend in the shipping business, and would see what the man could find out about the *Sea Hawk.*

This pleased Connie, and she began to eat her oatmeal. The conversation turned to plans for the water carnival to be held on the lake that afternoon.

Hal and Bert were to dress like Indians and paddle Hal's canoe. Their tanned faces and bodies were to be made even darker with theatrical powder. The Minturns' feather duster would be dissected to make the boys' headgear.

Harry was to be an explorer, standing in the craft. He was to represent Father Marquette, the discoverer of the upper Mississippi River.

It was simple to make Harry look like the famous explorer, for he was tall and dark, and the robes were easily arranged by using a black shawl, with a rough cord tied about his waist.

"Nan, why don't you go as Pocahontas, the beautiful Indian girl?" suggested Dorothy.

"Why don't you girls take another period of history?" asked Hal. "We can't all be Indians."

"Who was some famous girl or woman in American history?" asked Harry, glad to get a chance to stump Dorothy on her history.

"Oh, there are lots of them," answered the girl promptly. "Don't think that men were the only people in America who did anything worth while. How about Barbara Fritchie and Clara Barton, and—"

"Then be one you particularly admire," said Harry.

"Oh, let us be real," suggested Connie. "Everybody will be make-believe. I saw lots of people getting their boats ready when I went for a walk this morning. I'm sure they will look like Christmas-tree things; tinsel and paper and colored stuff."

"What would be real?" questioned Dorothy, puzzled.

"Well, the Fisherman's Daughters," Connie said slowly. "We have a picture at home of two little girls waiting—for their—father. Couldn't we do something like that?"

"I see what you mean," murmured Nan.

Surely it would be real for Connie to be a fisherman's daughter, waiting for her father!

"I have that picture in a book here," said Dorothy. "We can copy it exactly. And I know where we can borrow an old rowboat."

It had already been decided that Flossie, Freddie, and Dorothy should go in the Minturn boat, which was to be decorated like a Venetian gondola. Dorothy would be an Italian lady.

It was amazing how quickly and how well Nan managed to fix up her costume and Connie's. Of course, the boys made wonderful Indians, and Harry a splendid French explorer. Dorothy only had to wear a pretty dress and put lace and flowers on her head to make her look like a Venetian lady.

Freddie was a little prince in his black velvet suit with Flossie's red sash tied from his shoulder to his waist, in gay court fashion. Flossie wore the pink slip that belonged under her party dress. On her head was a silk handkerchief pinned up at the ends in that quaint square fashion of little girls of old Venice.

There were to be prizes for the best costumes and prettiest floats. The judges' stand was a very showy affair, built on the pier at one side of the lake.

There was plenty of excitement along the shore, too, for a large crowd had gathered to watch the procession lining up. A band was playing a gay tune.

The Minturn boat was given second place in the children's section, just back of the mayor's daughter, and the Bingham rowboat, skillfully transformed into an airplane by the lifeguard's young brother, came next.

In the long line were all kinds of boats, some made to represent impossible things like giant swans and eagles. In one, an automobile headlight had been put inside a great paper head which was intended to look like a monster sea serpent.

Colored wires were its fangs. The eyes blazed, and the red mouth stood wide open. There were horns made of twisted pieces of tin, and altogether the sea serpent looked very fierce indeed.

After the larger floats, most of them manned by grownups, the first of the smaller boats came along. The children in their gay costumes appeared.

"Father Marquette!" cried a man on shore, instantly recognizing the historic figure Harry represented.

How slowly the canoe came along, and how solemn the three boys looked! As they reached the judges' stand, Harry stood up and shaded his eyes with his hand, looking off in the distance, exactly like the picture of the famous French explorer.

This brought out long and loud cheering, and the boys deserved it, for they not only looked like the adventurous Frenchman and his Indian guides, but really acted the part.

There followed more small boats. In one was a pretty girl in a white satin bathing suit, holding a big red beach ball. In another sat a cowboy. There was also a craft fixed up to look like a small gunboat with wooden guns in which firecrackers were exploding.

Then came a boat in which several boys were dressed in the funny-looking, old-fashioned long bathing suits men used to wear. The boys seemed to be enjoying themselves even more than the people looking at them.

"Oh, look at this!" called a woman in the audience, as a battered old rowboat with two girls in it drifted along.

The Fisherman's Daughters!

Perhaps it was because there was so much gaiety about the other boats that Nan and Connie looked particularly impressive. From the side of their weather-beaten boat dragged an old fish net. Each girl wore a black hood, and from under hers, Connie's brown hair fell in tangles on her bare shoulders. The children wore bodices, like pictures of Dutch girls, and full skirts of dark material.

As they sat in the boat and looked out to sea, "watching for the fisherman's return," their anxious attitude and pose were perfect. The people on shore were so impressed that they seemed spellbound, and did not even clap at first.

"That child is an actress," said one woman, noting the look on Connie's face.

But Connie was not acting. She was lost in thought. When would her father come back to her?

After the last craft in the procession had passed the judges' stand, the contestants brought their floats around to face the judges on the pier. Everybody in the boats and on the shore anxiously waited to learn who would get the prizes.

CHAPTER XIV

A MYSTERY

FIRST came the prizes for the large floats, and the sea serpent was judged the funniest and awarded a prize. It seemed like a long wait before the various classes of smaller boats were called to go past the stand again. But at last a man called out through a megaphone:

"All children's boats please come past the judges again!"

So the children's parade started all over again. As the last boat passed, there was a consultation among the judges, then the announcer shouted:

"First prize goes to the most natural and most artistic group—the Fisherman's Daughters!"

"Oh!" cried Connie. This was the first prize she had ever won!

She and Nan rowed over and were handed a small silver treasure chest. Inside was an order from one of the stores for twenty-five dollars' worth of clothes.

"I—I just can't believe it," said Connie. "Thank you so much."

The onlookers clapped their hands in approval and shouted for the girls to pose once more as the Fisherman's Daughters. Nan and Connie gladly played their parts once more, and the people along the shore clapped louder than ever. Finally the head judge stood up to make another announcement.

Second prize went to Marquette and the Indians. The boys were overjoyed.

"Golly, are we lucky!" Bert said to Hal. "I hope they don't mind that our family is getting more than one prize," he added, as they rowed off, each boy with a pair of clipper-ship bookends.

The third prize went to the bathing girl, and the fourth to the gunboat crew. Everybody seemed pleased and the clapping continued a long time.

Perfect weather had added to the success of the water carnival, and now most of the people started for the pavilion where there was to be a party. The place was gaily decorated with banners, and tables laden with wonderful things to eat had been set up.

"Mother," said Nan, coming up to her, "I think Connie should keep the whole prize. I really have all the clothes I need."

"That's a fine idea," Mrs. Bobbsey agreed, "and perhaps we might add something to it for her mother."

The mayor's wife, Mrs. Blake, came over to the table where Mrs. Minturn, Mrs. Bobbsey, Aunt Sarah, and Mrs. Bingham were sitting.

"Mrs. Minturn, who was the lovely little girl with Nan Bobbsey?" she asked, as she sat down. "I don't remember seeing her before."

Mrs. Minturn told the story about Connie's father, and how the child had come to the seashore to build up strength. At once the mayor's wife became sympathetic, and offered to add to the prize.

She spoke quietly to several of her friends, and when Connie opened the treasure chest the next time, there were ten five-dollar bills in an envelope with her name on it.

"Why—why where did this come from?" she gasped.

Nan giggled. "A fairy put it there, I guess," she said.

Connie did not smile. She knew the Bobbseys and Minturns had had a lot to do with it. Such wonderful friends!

"Everyone's so sweet," she said. "If I take this, Nan, you must take the prize."

"No, no," Nan insisted. Then, seeing the hurt look on Connie's face, she added, "Suppose I take the treasure chest, and you take the rest. I'd love to have the chest on my dresser for bracelets and necklaces."

"Please do," Connie murmured softly.

"Speaking of fairies," said Mrs. Bobbsey, "we ought to show Connie the Fairy Castle."

"Oh yes," agreed Nan. "Let's go tomorrow afternoon."

She told Connie what had happened when they were there the time before. Maybe they could solve the mystery this time!

"I'd love to go," said Connie. "Only I thought maybe I ought to go back to the city and give this money to my mother."

Aunt Emily said she was sure a few days would make no difference, and the money could be mailed just as well.

"And we want you to stay here," Mrs. Minturn smiled.

When the carnival festivities were over, and the Bobbseys and their friends had eaten so much that they had to call it their supper, they went home. The children were so excited that they had a hard time falling asleep that night.

Nan, who was still awake long after Dorothy, thought she heard sounds in the room above. Was Connie up? Was she feeling sad again, maybe crying? Nan decided to go up and find out.

Quietly getting out of bed, Nan tiptoed upstairs and opened the door to Connie's room. There she was, sitting on the edge of her bed near the window, looking out at the sea!

"Connie, can't you sleep?" asked Nan, sitting down beside her friend. "Are you thinking about your father?"

"Yes, I am. But it's all right, Nan, I'm not sad tonight," Connie replied. "I don't know whether it was the wonderful thing that happened to me today, but I have a feeling my father *is* still alive and that I'm going to see him again someday."

"Oh, that's wonderful," said Nan. She kissed Connie and went downstairs again.

At this moment, Mr. and Mrs. Minturn, Mrs. Bobbsey, and Aunt Sarah were in the Binghams' living room, talking about the missing *Sea Hawk*.

"There is no doubt about it," Mr. Bingham said. "Connie's father sailed on my brother's ship. Poor girl, I'm afraid we can't hold out hope much longer."

"Oh, if only the *Sea Hawk* might be reported!" said Mrs. Bobbsey. "My husband is trying to find out something about it."

"I've exhausted every possibility I know," sighed Hal Bingham's father.

"What was it that your brother and Mr. McLaughlin went to get?" Mrs. Bobbsey asked.

"A cargo of rare teakwood," Mr. Bingham replied. "The cargo was worth a fortune, for it was carefully selected wood, and was to fill a special order in this country. If the *Sea Hawk* should ever come in, Connie's father would be comparatively rich."

"And your brother, too, of course," said Mrs. Bobbsey. "Let us hope with all our hearts that there will soon be some news of the *Sea Hawk*. There's an old saying that 'No news is good news,' and since you have heard nothing, perhaps the freighter has been stranded on some lonely island, and will turn up one of these days."

Mr. Bingham smiled hopefully, and for a few moments no one spoke. Then Mrs. Bingham came into the room, carrying a tray of lemonade and homemade cookies. The conversation turned to lighter matters, including the plan to visit the Fairy Castle the next day.

"Has Hal been there?" Aunt Emily asked.

His mother said he had, and that he knew the secret about the fairy.

"You know," said Mrs. Bingham, "everyone who learns the secret is asked not to tell it to anyone else."

"Yes, I know," said Aunt Emily. "Dorothy found out about the fairy last summer."

For this reason Dorothy and Hal did not go with Mrs. Bobbsey and the others the next day when they set off for the Fairy Castle. Bert was determined that he was going to solve the mystery this time.

When they drove up to the castlelike playhouse, no one was around. As before, the key was hanging by the door with an invitation to visitors to use it. Hopefully, Bert opened the door and they all walked inside.

They went at once into the room where the fairy had been standing in front of the fireplace. This time the curtain was pulled down.

"Maybe the fairy's behind the curtain," said Flossie. "Please, Nan, come with me and let's look."

All the children walked on tiptoe toward the curtain. Flossie was the first one to peek behind it.

"Oh!" she cried.

Bert pulled the curtain aside just in time to hear a voice say:

"Catch me if you can!"

Two small slippered feet were just disappearing up the chimney!

"The fairy! She's gone up the chimney!" cried Freddie.

Bert already had dashed forward and was looking up the chimney. He could see nothing but a bit of blue sky above.

"She's gone!" he cried.

"She said to catch her!" exclaimed Freddie excitedly.

"That's an idea. Come on, Harry, let's try to find the fairy!" said Bert.

As the boys' eyes became accustomed to the chimney, they could see little steps leading up the side. Quickly they mounted them and came to a little door. Bert pushed it and stepped onto a little balcony. Steps led down from it to the ground.

The fairy was not in sight. Where was she hiding?

Bert ran down the steps to the ground and around the side of the house, Harry close at his heels. They still did not see the fairy.

Inside the house there was great excitement.

The other Bobbsey children and Connie were running from one place to another. Mrs. Bobbsey was smiling broadly, but she, too, had been fooled. After the fairy disappeared, she had looked out in the hall, fully expecting a child to run in and race up the stairway. But this time no one entered the house.

"She must have run off outdoors," Mrs. Bobbsey told herself. "Maybe the boys will see her."

But Bert and Harry did not see a fairy or a little girl or any other person. They came into the house and talked the puzzle over with the others.

"She must be one of Santa Claus's fairies," Flossie declared.

"Why?" Nan asked.

" 'Cause she went up the chimney," said Flossie.

Freddie was inclined to agree with his sister, but the others smiled. Bert ran outside again and looked down the road and across the fields that bordered the playhouse. Seeing no one, he suddenly had an idea that the fairy might have gone all the way up the chimney and was hiding in some secret place on the roof.

He returned to the house and went up the little steps inside the chimney again. But he could not find any steps going higher, so he climbed down again, completely mystified about the whole thing.

"I guess the fairy doesn't like us," said Freddie, heaving a great big sigh.

"I guess not," his mother agreed. "Well, suppose we go home."

"Oh, please, Mother, not yet," Nan pleaded. "Let's start all over again and maybe we will see the fairy. I think we ran in too fast and she wasn't ready for us."

"That's an idea," her mother agreed. "We'll do that."

The Bobbseys, Connie, and Harry hurried outside, locked the door, hung up the key, and walked to their car. Then they turned around and went back to the Fairy Castle. This time they opened the door slowly, walked in very quietly, and entered the room where they hoped the fairy would be. The curtain was open and there stood the fairy in front of the fireplace!

"Come!" she said in her high, tiny voice. "Have you any wishes you would like me to carry to the queen of the fairies?"

Freddie and Flossie were still a little frightened and did not move. They clung to their mother's hands. But finally Freddie spoke up and said:

"I want a new fire engine!"

"Your wish shall be granted," said the fairy.

"And I want a big new doll!" cried Flossie excitedly.

"At Christmas your wish shall be granted," said the fairy. "And now, will you and your little brother please wait outside my castle while I hear the wishes of these other children?"

Mrs. Bobbsey took the small twins back to the car. Not once did they ask whether or not the fairy was real. Both of them were too busy thinking about the new fire engine and the big doll they had been promised.

Inside the playhouse castle, the other three children were learning the fairy's secret. As soon as Freddie and Flossie had left, the fairy held out her hand and said:

"Come! I am a real person!"

Nan was the first one to walk up. She was even more amazed than before. For a moment she had thought this was a little girl playing the part of a fairy. Now she realized that she was looking at the tiniest woman she had ever seen!

Then Bert, Harry, and Connie came up. Bert grinned.

"Where were you hiding?" he asked.

The fairylike woman said the playhouse had many doors, and she could run down from the balcony and enter the castle without being seen.

"But your mother saw me last time you were here," the little lady smiled. "She was a dear not to give me away. I was a bit afraid the small twins could not keep my secret, so that was why I asked them to leave."

Nan asked how long the little lady had been playing the part of a fairy. She said almost ever since the playhouse had been built. The man who had made it for his children had thought up the little scheme and engaged her. What years and years of pleasure she had had playing the part!

"Do you always tell children their wishes will come true?" Connie asked her.

The little lady said that it was only when children wished for something that would be good for them, and when she thought it was possible for their parents to see that the wishes were granted, that she told them the wishes would come true.

Nan and Bert knew that Connie had a great big wish in her mind, and how hard they hoped it would come true!

CHAPTER XV

PLAYING ROBINSON CRUSOE

NEXT morning Freddie and Flossie were up early, and went outdoors while they were waiting for breakfast. They talked about the fairy, trying to figure out where she came from and where she went. And they hoped she was right about their wishes coming true.

"Good morning! Good morning!" said Uncle William, joining them. "And how are my little sailors today?"

The small twins stared. Then Freddie said, "I'm a fireman."

"Not today." Uncle William grinned. "All I have to do is say, 'One, two, three,' and you're both sailors."

Bringing one hand from behind his back, he held up a large toy sailboat. It had three masts and several sails.

"Is this for us?" gasped Freddie.

"Yes," Uncle William smiled. "And I'll tell

you where to sail it—down on the little cove in the lake where the Binghams' new rowboat is."

He held his finger up, and said the wind was blowing just right for their game. They could send their ship out on one side of the cove, and walk around to the other side and get it.

"Oh thank you, Uncle William," said first Flossie, then Freddie.

They wanted to start the game at once, but of course they had to eat breakfast. During the meal they had no chance to mention their gift, and then they started out almost directly afterward. Halfway to the pond, Flossie said:

"We forgot to tell Mommy where we're going."

"Uncle William knows," Freddie replied.

But Uncle William did not think to tell anyone, and left for the city. In the meantime, Freddie and Flossie had arrived at the cove with their new sailboat.

They set it in the water and at once it started for the other side of the cove. It went very fast.

"Boy, it's a dandy boat," said Freddie, starting to run along the shore to get it.

After he had had two turns, Flossie let it go, and away the boat sailed, faster than ever! A little later she said:

"Let's play carnival, and decorate the boat."

"With what?" asked Freddie.

"Oh—leaves—and maybe some flowers," his twin answered.

"Okay," replied Freddie.

Together they walked to a near-by woods and started hunting for decorations. Freddie found some leaves, while Flossie picked several pretty bluebells. They laid them on the deck of the sailboat and looked at it proudly.

"I think this would have won a prize in the boat parade," said Freddie.

"Maybe first prize," agreed Flossie. Then she giggled. "But you would have had to sit in it, and you're too big—the boat would have drowned."

"Boats don't drown," said Freddie. "They sink!"

"Well, it's better to play carnival this way," answered Flossie, setting the boat on the water and giving it a little push.

Now while the two little sailors had been playing, something had happened which they did not know about. The wind had changed!

The next instant the little boat made a turn with the breeze, and before Flossie or Freddie could grab it, the boat headed out into the lake.

"Oh, our boat!" Freddie cried. "Get it, quick!"

"I can't!" declared Flossie. "It's out too far! Oh, what shall we do?"

"You were the captain and you shouldn't have let it go," Freddie scolded. "You'll have to get it!"

But poor Flossie could not reach the boat.

"Oh, it's going far away!" she cried, almost in tears.

The little boat was certainly making its way fast out into the lake, as if it were glad to be free.

"There's Hal Bingham's boat," ventured Flossie. "Maybe we could borrow it to get our sailboat."

"Of course we can," promptly answered Freddie. "I know how to row."

"But we've never been out alone before," Flossie said, hesitating.

"Oh, it's not deep here," her brother assured her.

This assurance gave the little girl courage. Very carefully Flossie got into the back seat. Then Freddie climbed in, slipped the rope off a large peg that secured the boat to the shore, and took the middle seat.

The oars were so big that Freddie found he could not work them both at the same time. When he pulled back on just one oar, the boat only went around in circles. He tried again and again, but each time the boat went around, and the oar seemed to get heavier and heavier.

He finally gave one last yank on the oar. It skimmed the surface of the water. Flossie let out a yell as she was splashed from head to toe. At the same time, Freddie fell backward off his seat into the bottom of the boat.

"Freddie Bobbsey!" Flossie laughed. Her brother looked very funny with his legs sticking up straight in the air. "You don't know how to row at all."

"I do so!" said Freddie sternly. "It's just that these oars are too big."

He decided not to use the oars and pulled them inside the boat.

"We'll paddle with our hands," suggested Freddie. "You paddle on one side and I'll paddle on the other."

"Isn't this lovely!" Flossie declared a few minutes later, as the boat moved quietly along.

"We're not moving very fast," said Freddie. "Can you see the sailboat?"

"Yes. But, Freddie, how are we going to get back?" asked Flossie, beginning to worry. The wind was carrying them rather far from shore.

"Oh, easy!" replied Freddie, who began to feel brave. After all, he was captain of the boat.

"The tide comes in pretty soon, and then this boat will go back to shore with it."

Freddie had heard so much about the tide, he felt he understood it perfectly. Of course there was no tide in the lake, but Freddie did not know that.

"Oh," he complained suddenly, looking around, "we're not getting near the sailboat."

"Well, I can't help it," said Flossie. "I wish we could go back to shore in a hurry. I'm going to call somebody."

"Nobody will hear you," said her brother. "They're all down by the ocean and that's a long way from here."

"But I want to go home, Freddie!" cried Flossie.

"Oh, all right," said her twin brother, annoyed at his sister. Now he would never find the sailboat.

While both children tried very hard to paddle with their hands, the rowboat kept drifting farther and farther from the shore. It was headed around a bend in the lake, where there was a little island. This was entirely out of view of either the Minturn or the Bingham boat landings.

"Look, Freddie!" exclaimed Flossie. "An island!"

"Oh, we'll be Robinson Crusoes!" he answered excitedly, delighted at the prospect of such an adventure.

"I don't want to be Robinson Crusoe!" pouted his sister. "I just want to get back home," and she began to cry.

"Don't cry," said Freddie, feeling sorry for his twin. "Maybe we'll find someone to help us."

"How?"

Freddie did not answer this. Instead, he said, "We're going to bump."

At that the rowboat did bump into the shore of the little island.

"Come, Flossie, let's be explorers, and see what's on this island."

"Be careful!" she cautioned. "Don't step out till I get hold of your hand. It's awfully easy to slip getting out of a boat."

Once on land, Flossie's fears left her, and she told Freddie she would not mind playing Robinson Crusoe with him for a while.

"I'm going to build a hut," said Freddie, picking up some pieces of dry wood and standing them against a tree. "You can be my man Friday and help me."

The small twins became so interested in their hut that they did not notice what was happening to the rowboat. In their eagerness to get ashore, they had forgotten to pull it up on land. Now it was drifting away. They could not get off the island!

They played for about half an hour, then Flossie said she was tired of the game. She did not like being the man Friday and waiting on Freddie all the time.

"I think we should try to go home," she said.

"Yes, it must be lunchtime. I'm hungry," agreed Freddie. "Let's find the boat."

The little twins walked back to the water's edge and to their amazement, could find no boat.

"But—but where could it go?" asked Freddie.

"Now what'll we do?" wailed Flossie.

"There's someone!" cried Freddie, pointing to a man who was rowing toward them. "Hello!" Freddie shouted. "Will you help us get to land?"

"Freddie!" exclaimed Flossie. "He's pulling a boat! Maybe it's ours!"

As the man came closer, the twins could see that he looked very friendly; in fact, he had a great big grin on his pleasant, round face.

"Well, youngsters," he said, "did you lose this boat?"

"Yes, we did," admitted Freddie. "We forgot to tie it up."

"We can't row it," added Flossie. "The oars

are too heavy. Can you help us get back to our house?"

"Of course I'll help you," offered the nice man. "My name is Smith. What's yours?"

"Freddie Bobbsey," spoke up the little boy. "This is my twin Flossie and we're staying at Aunt Emily Minturn's."

"You are, eh? Then it was your brother that my cow brought home from the woods when he was lost," said the man. "Do you Bobbseys get lost often?" he joked.

Carefully he lifted the twins into his boat. Then he started rowing to the dock from which the children had started.

"If you have a cow, you're a farmer, aren't you?" said Flossie presently.

"Reckon I am!" laughed the man.

"Then you couldn't be a sailor," she sighed.

"What's on your mind, little lady?" Mr. Smith asked.

"Our sailboat. We lost it."

The man asked where and how big the toy sailboat was. When he heard it was new and very pretty, the nice farmer said:

"We'll look for it right away!"

CHAPTER XVI

THE WITCH'S BIRD

THE KIND farmer turned the rowboat around, and the twins started looking for their lost sailboat.

"Let's see, the wind is blowing from the south," Mr. Smith said, "so we'll go over that way first."

He nodded toward the shore beyond the island, where the woods came down to the water's edge. As he rowed along, Freddie suddenly cried out:

"I see it! I see it!"

The little boy stood up and began to jump up and down with glee.

"Sit down, young man!" the farmer ordered sternly. "You're rocking the boat. You'll dump us all in the water."

Freddie sat down, but he had a hard time keeping still, for they were getting nearer and

124

nearer the sailboat. In a few moments he was able to reach out his hand and pick it up. The leaves and flowers were still on deck.

"It *is* a nice boat," Mr. Smith agreed. "I'm glad we found it. And now I'd better take you home. Your folks are probably wondering where you are."

Indeed, Mrs. Bobbsey and the others were worried. They had been down to the beach, over to the pond, and into the woods.

Bert and Nan had just come down to the lake to look. And here were their small brother and sister coming across the water in a boat, laughing and talking just as if nothing had happened!

"Oh, you're all right," called out Nan in relief.

"Course we're all right," said Flossie.

"We played Robinson Crusoe on an island!" cried Freddie, getting out of the boat.

"I was his man Friday," announced Flossie. "And we had to wait till somebody rescued us."

Of course it did not take long to clear up the mystery of the little twins' disappearance. Bert and Nan thanked the farmer for his kindness in rescuing the twins and the sailboat and the Binghams' rowboat. Then Mr. Smith rowed off, waving his hand, and the Bobbseys went home.

"You must never go out in a boat alone again,"

Mrs. Bobbsey told Flossie and Freddie, when they reached the house. "Not until you are older, and know how to handle a boat."

"We're sorry," said the twins together.

They certainly had never thought of all the things that could have happened to them. How lucky they were to be safe again, they decided.

Aunt Sarah and Harry were to have left for Meadow Brook early that morning, but the worry over the children had delayed them, and Aunt Emily prevailed upon them to stay another day.

Harry was very glad to hear this. Directly after lunch he, Bert, and Hal started for the woods at the end of the lake. They were going to hunt for white birch trees. Hal knew how to make small Indian canoes from the bark. The boys had decided to try making a canoe for Bert to use, so he could have races with Hal on the lake.

As they entered the woods, a mist blew in from the ocean. Floating layers of it surrounded the boys in a few minutes.

"Say, this is spooky," said Bert. "Do you suppose we ought to turn back? We can't see much ahead."

"No, this mist will disappear all of a sudden," replied Hal. "Then we can find the birch trees."

As the boys stood waiting, Bert let out a yell. Something had whisked past his face.

"What's the matter?" cried Harry.

Bert laughed. "It was only a bird, but it scared me. We must have disturbed the old fellow."

"There it is!" exclaimed Hal, pointing to a flurry of brilliant feathers. "What is it?"

"Boy, the bird's big," said Harry. "Queer looking, too. I never saw anything like it before."

The boys tried to get a better look at the bird. One minute they could see it plainly and the next it would disappear into the thin veil of mist.

"Look!" said Bert.

The odd bird had rested for a moment on a tree close by. It pecked at the bark as if trying to play a tune. Each time its beak struck the bark, the bird's head bobbed up and down in a peculiar fashion.

"It's not a woodpecker," remarked Hal, "but it sure pecks like one."

"I wish we could catch it," said Bert, but the bird had already disappeared again.

A few minutes later the mist cleared, and the boys looked for the bird, but it remained out of sight. Finally they went on to gather the birch wood for a canoe.

"Let's start work on the boat right away," said Bert when they reached home.

By suppertime they had the frame built. Then the three boys went for a dip in the ocean, and hurried home just as the Minturns' sea bell rang, announcing the evening meal. The strange bird the boys had seen was much talked about all evening, everyone trying to guess what it might be.

"Maybe it's a witch's bird," declared Dinah jokingly.

"Oooh!" said Freddie, his eyes opening wide. "What's a witch's bird?"

"It's like a ghost's bird, only different," put in Dorothy, laughing.

Dorothy liked anything spooky, and she was never happier than when she was playing a trick on someone. Now she was trying to confuse little Freddie and Flossie.

"Tell us more, Dinah. What does a witch's bird do?" asked Flossie.

"Well," said Dinah in a very soft voice, "a witch's bird sometimes brings messages to people—sort of warns them about things that are goin' to happen."

"That's right," said Dorothy. "They are scary, though—you can never tell what they might do!"

"Such stories!" laughed Bert. "A witch's bird couldn't scare me!"

"Well, you can never tell, child," said Dinah. "Maybe that witch's bird will visit you tonight.

When you hear a funny rat-a-tat-tat, then you'll know it's the witch's bird bringing you a strange message."

After the small twins had gone to bed, the older children sat on the porch and talked. Bert and Harry kept teasing the girls about ghosts and witches. They made all kinds of weird sounds and howled with laughter when Nan pretended to be scared and ran to hide.

Finally the young folks went to bed, and then the grownups. By ten o'clock the house was quiet. Somewhat later—it must have been midnight, for Bert was positive he had just heard the clock strike twelve—there came a queer sound at his window. It was a pecking sound!

"I must be dreaming," Bert thought. "Dinah's story about a witch's bird tapping on my window can't be true."

Bert shut his eyes tight and turned over. There was not a sound for a minute and then—

Rat-a-tat-tat! Rat-a-tat-tat!

Now Bert's heart began to pound! He sat up in bed, and looked all around the room, then out the window. He could see nothing.

"Harry! Harry!" he called softly to his cousin. "Wake up!"

"Wha—what's the matter?" asked Harry sleepily.

"I heard a strange noise," answered Bert. "A funny tapping noise."

"Golly, do you suppose it really is a witch's bird?" whispered Harry. "Dinah said it would bring us a message. I thought she was only teasing us."

"Shssh!" said Bert. "There it is again. Don't light the lamp," he cautioned. "I'll crawl over to the window."

Bert ran across the room to the window and quickly stuck his head out.

"There's nothing here!" he whispered excitedly to Harry. "I'm sure the noise came from this side of the house."

No sooner was Bert comfortably settled in bed again when the spooky noise started once more. This time it was much louder.

"There it is again!" called Bert. "I'll get him this time!"

Grabbing a tennis racket, he quickly crawled out on the porch roof, which was just outside the window.

"Do you see anything?" asked Harry.

"No!" shouted Bert, forgetting it was very late. "Say, did you hear somebody laughing just now?"

"No," answered Harry. "Are you—"

"What's the matter up there?" called Dinah

from her bedroom window below. "You're makin' a powerful lot of noise. Can't you let nobody get a wink of sleep?"

"I'm sorry, Dinah," said Bert. "Were you laughing just a moment ago?"

"Laughin'?" Dinah questioned. "What's ailin' you, Bert? With all that noise upstairs, do you think I'd be laughin' this time of night?"

Both Bert and Harry were on the roof now in their pajamas.

"What's—the—matter?" called Connie in a very drowsy voice from her window on the third floor.

"What are you boys after?" called Uncle William from a middle window.

"Golly," said Bert, "everybody's awake now!"

"Anything wrong?" asked Aunt Sarah anxiously.

"We're all right," said Bert. "We thought we heard something, but I guess we were wrong."

After the boys had gone back into their room, Bert whispered to Harry, "I'm going to Uncle William's room and tell him what we heard. Maybe he knows what it was."

Bert quietly walked down the hall to his uncle's room. Uncle William listened intently to Bert's story.

"Hm—a tapping sound on the window," he

said. "I have an idea, Bert. We'll go upstairs to the attic and see if we can find this witch's bird."

Bert, mystified, quietly followed his uncle upstairs to the attic. They tiptoed over to a closed storage room. Uncle William cautiously turned the knob of the door and flung it open.

"You think it was a bat?" suggested Bert.

"No, I don't think so," answered his uncle. "Listen! I think I hear girls laughing!" At that moment an audible giggle was heard from the far side of the room.

Quickly Uncle William reached for a chain in the middle of the room and pulled it. Light flooded the room.

"There are two witch's birds," he said, laughing.

Standing over in a corner near a window were Nan and Dorothy. They did not know whether to laugh or cry after being caught.

"How did you make that pecking sound?" asked Bert, puzzled. He ran to the open window and looked out. Nothing there.

"Own up, girls," said Uncle William, chuckling.

Dorothy brought her hands from behind her back. In them she held a tick-tack. The string was long, and on the end was a nail. She had swung it out the window against the one below.

"So that's how you made the noise on our window," said Bert, disgusted at himself for not having guessed the trick.

"We didn't mean to wake up the whole house," said Nan. "We just thought we'd scare Bert and Harry."

"Well, it was a good trick," declared Uncle William, chuckling. "Now let's put the ghosts and witch's bird out of our minds and get back to bed."

They all trooped downstairs. But Bert and Harry did not go to sleep at once. They were planning how to get even with the girls the next morning.

"I know a good trick," said Harry, and whispered something to Bert.

Then both boys went to sleep.

CHAPTER XVII

THE RESCUE

BERT and Harry were up early next morning. They asked for breakfast before the others were served, and said they were going off to finish the birch bark canoe.

"How about a swim?" asked Dorothy, who liked to play with the boys.

"We'll meet you at ten-thirty," called Bert. He winked at Harry as they went down the path toward Hal's garage, where they were building the canoe.

When the girls arrived at the beach later, the boys were already there, dressed in their swimming shorts. Nan, Dorothy, and Connie went into the Minturns' big bathhouse. Two minutes later squeals of annoyance came from inside. The boys listened, their eyes twinkling.

"I can't get into this suit!"

"Mine's sewed up tight!"

There was a shriek. "Whee-ee, a mouse!"

Silence for several seconds. Then Dorothy cried out, "Bert and Harry! They did this!"

The boys grinned. Then, before the girls could take the stitches out of their sewn-up bathing suits, Bert, Harry, and Hal had run down to the water and dived in.

But one fact the boys had not counted on. Their clothes were in the next bathhouse, and when they went to dress after their swim, every bit of clothing was tied in knots!

"Fellows," said Harry, as he struggled with his shirt, "the girls are still one trick ahead of us. Let's even the score."

"Sure thing," Bert and Hal agreed.

Nan suspected that her twin would not let the matter rest there, so she and the other girls watched carefully for another joke. But the day wore on and nothing happened.

Just before supper Bert suggested that the donkeys should be exercised. He offered to hitch them to the cart and drive out on the beach.

"Harry and I'll take a ride," he said, "and then you girls can take a turn. We'll call you."

"All right," Dorothy answered, and added to Nan and Connie, "we'll take a long ride on the sand. I'll show you the Coast Guard station."

About twenty minutes later, the girls heard

their names called and hurried down to the beach. The boys hopped out of the cart and the three girls climbed in. Dorothy took the reins.

"Giddap!" she said, slapping Doodle and Dandy gently with the lines. "Run!"

Doodle and Dandy did run—but all by themselves. They yanked the reins from Dorothy's hands, and galloped down the beach without the cart.

The shaft dropped to the sand with a thud and the three girls tumbled forward in their seats.

"Have a nice ride!" yelled Hal, as the boys ran toward the house.

Nan and Connie laughed, but Dorothy said, "I'll fix those boys! The donkeys won't come back by themselves. They'll just wait until I go and get them."

"We'll all go," said Nan, and the three girls started off across the sand.

The animals were still running, and seemed to be enjoying their freedom. Their young owner and her friends had a long walk before reaching them, so no time was left for a ride.

"I guess we're even," Nan told her twin as they came to the table, and he nodded.

The evening was quiet, for all the children went to bed early after a strenuous day. Moreover, several friends from Meadow Brook were to arrive the next morning to spend the day on the beach. Bert and Harry had said they would go down early to the ocean and pick up any driftwood or seaweed that might have cluttered the beach during the night.

Hal joined them. Soon they had collected a large pile of wood to cart away directly after breakfast. When the boys were about to leave, Bert said:

"Listen! I thought I heard a cry for help!"

The sound was very faint, but Bert was sure he had heard someone call. Then, out among the waves, he spotted a man's bobbing head.

"Help!" came the call again.

"That man's in trouble!" Bert shouted to Hal and Harry. "Come on!"

All three kicked off their shoes, and dived in. The man had disappeared, but the boys swam to where they had last seen him.

"I'll dive down!" shouted Bert.

Hal and Harry looked toward the shore for help, hoping the lifeguard might have come on duty. The boys knew they would need all the assistance they could get if Bert did not find the man in a hurry!

Bert's head appeared above the water. "I've got him!" he gasped. "Help me! He—"

Under the water Bert went. He had hold of a

large man, who was struggling to hang on to him.

"He's pulling Bert down!" cried Hal. Then he dived under with Harry.

The three boys came to the top with the man, but what a struggle he put up!

"I'll have to break his hold on Bert," Harry decided in desperation.

He aimed a blow at the side of the man's face. It surprised the man so that he let go of Bert's neck.

"We'll get you in," cried Bert. "But don't grab anyone!"

The man seemed to recover from his fright, and the boys towed him to shore. As the four staggered up onto the beach, a lifeguard, who was just coming on duty, ran down to the water's edge to meet them.

"You boys sure did a wonderful job," he said, seeing that the man was not hurt. "Are you all right, Mr. Cole?"

"Yes—I—think so. They—saved—my life!" he gasped. "Had a cramp—in—my leg. Lost—my head. They—brought me up—almost—from—the bottom!"

"I'd better have someone drive you home," suggested the young guard.

"Yes—thank you."

Several people had gathered by this time, and

one man, who had a car, offered to take Mr. Cole home. The others crowded around the three young rescuers.

"We didn't hear any cry for help," said one man. "It's a good thing you boys did."

"They deserve a medal," said another.

"How did it happen?" asked a woman.

Bert, Hal, and Harry told the group how they had saved the man, and smilingly acknowledged the praise they received. After a while the boys became embarrassed, and decided to go home.

Each of them had to explain his wet clothes and tell the story again. Dinah walked back and forth fanning herself with her apron.

"Oh my! Oh my!" she kept saying. "Those boys, they might 'a' been drowned. But no, they just run right into that big ocean and didn't mind nothin'. They're sure brave boys!"

"Please stop!" Bert begged. "Anyone would have done the same thing."

"No sir, no sir," Dinah insisted, and so they let her have her own way about it.

The boys were glad when it was time for their friends from Meadow Brook to arrive. A large bus brought the men, women, and children from the station to the beach. As the Bobbsey twins and their cousins hurried across the sand to meet them, Bert said:

"I hope Jack Hopkins came." Jack had been one of his best friends at Meadow Brook.

"Oh, he'll be along," Harry remarked. "And August Stout."

"There they are!" cried Bert, as a group of shouting, laughing children, carrying picnic baskets, ran toward the ocean.

"Hello there! Hello there!" called everybody at once, for, of course, all the children knew Harry and many also knew Bert.

Tom Mason was with them, and a number of girls, most of them friends of Nan's.

"Look! Here comes Uncle Daniel!" called Bert.

Sure enough, down to the beach came Uncle Daniel Bobbsey, with Nan holding one arm, and Dorothy clinging to the other, while Connie carried his small bag.

"I didn't even have a chance to get up to the house to see the folks," laughed Uncle Daniel, joining the boys. "These gals just dragged me down here. How's everybody?"

"Oh, we're fine," Nan assured him. "And won't Aunt Sarah be surprised! She never dreamed that you were coming! She almost went home with Harry. Oh, Uncle Daniel, we're so glad you came!"

"I am, too," he said. "Well, Harry, you're as

brown as an Indian. Can you see through that coat of tan?"

Harry laughed and said he certainly had been having a whale of a time. No sooner had his father sat down on the sand, when a small boy jumped on his back. Uncle Daniel was so surprised he let out a yell, which amused everybody.

Of course it was Freddie. He was so overjoyed at seeing his uncle that he had leaped at him without thinking of his weight.

"Freddie boy!" exclaimed Uncle Daniel, giving his nephew a good long hug. "And you have turned Indian, too! Where's the sea serpent you were going to catch for me?"

"I'll get him yet," declared the little fellow. "It hasn't rained hardly since we came down, and they only come in to land on rainy days."

This explanation made Uncle Daniel laugh heartily. Before he had a chance to go to the house, Aunt Sarah came to the beach. She was surprised and glad to see her husband.

When Flossie joined the group, she said it was like being in the country and at the seashore all at the same time. And what fun that was!

"There's Nettie Prentice!" exclaimed Nan suddenly. She spied her little country friend looking through the crowd, evidently searching for friends.

"Oh, Nan!" called Nettie in delight. "I'm so glad to see you all again. And the ocean, it's beautiful!"

"We'll have a perfectly wonderful time," declared Nan. "Dorothy, my cousin, is so much fun, and she has two donkeys and a cart. We'll take a ride."

Everybody proceeded to have just as much fun as he could squeeze into the few hours before the excursion train would leave on its return trip to Meadow Brook.

Bright beach umbrellas were set up on the sand to help keep the older folks from becoming too sunburned. The boys and girls played in the water, dug wells and trenches, and built sand castles, until one of the men called:

"Time for lunch!"

Such hurrying and scurrying, as children and grownups came from all directions! The picnic baskets had been set in a big circle and hardly anyone could wait until they were opened.

Mrs. Minturn had had lunches made for her family, so that they might spend most of the day on the beach with their friends. Flossie bit into a large, highly seasoned sandwich intended for Harry's father, and made a wry face.

"L-let's eat somebody else's lunch," she said,

tears in her eyes, and afraid all the sandwiches would be peppery.

At once two girls from Meadow Brook, Mabel and Mildred, handed over two dainty sandwiches.

"I've got a half and a half," Flossie said, drying her tears.

"What's a half and a half?" asked Freddie.

"A half chicken sandwich and a half peanut butter sandwich," she answered.

The others laughed.

"They *are* small," said Mabel, and handed over another sandwich.

"That was quite a deal," chuckled Uncle Daniel. "You'll make a good businesswoman when you grow up, Flossie!"

At this moment Bert happened to look across the sand. The lifeguard was striding toward them. In his hand he carried three packages.

The young man bent over and whispered something to several people. At once they got up and followed him. Bert heard one of them say, "They did?"

The boy wondered what all the excitement was about.

"There they are!" said the lifeguard, smiling at the Bobbseys and their friends.

Questions came from every direction. "Hal, why didn't you tell us you boys saved a man's life this morning?" asked an Ocean Cliff man.

"Think of that!" exclaimed a woman from Meadow Brook. "Three young boys rescuing a drowning man!"

The three boys stood together, amazed at all the sudden attention they were receiving. With the excitement of the beach picnic, they had forgotten about the event of the morning.

"I have several awards to make," said the lifeguard. "Will Bert and Harry Bobbsey and Hal Bingham please step up here?"

CHAPTER XVIII

THE UNDERGROUND CITY

THE LIFEGUARD smiled at the three boys.
Then he said:

"Mr. Cole, the man whose life you saved, has
asked me to present to each one of you a gift as a
token of his appreciation."

"But we don't expect any reward," spoke up
Bert.

"Mr. Cole knows that," replied the lifeguard.
"But he said you deserve a reward for being so
brave. He would have come to present it himself, but he couldn't make it today, and we understand Harry is leaving this afternoon."

"That's right," said Harry.

"Mr. Cole wants you boys to accept these with
his thanks," the lifeguard went on.

He handed a small package to each of the
boys.

"It's all right, son," said Mrs. Bobbsey, as Bert

145

looked questioningly at his mother. "You did a good deed, and I'm sure Mr. Cole is happy to give you a reward."

"It's a watch!" exclaimed Bert, opening his package.

"So is mine!" exclaimed Hal.

"I have one, too!" shouted Harry.

The boys thanked the lifeguard and said they would write their thanks to Mr. Cole. The crowd cheered, happy that the boys had received such fine rewards.

There was so much to do and so much to see that the few hours allowed the excursionists slipped by all too quickly. Dorothy got her donkey cart and gave Nettie Prentice and a few of the other girls a ride along the beach. The boys went for a last dip in the water.

A little later, the people began heading for the bus to take them to the station. Harry and Aunt Sarah already had packed, and had little to do at Aunt Emily's before starting.

Hal and Bert were sorry to see Harry go. He was a lot of fun and so good at sports, and he knew so much about plants and animals.

"Now, Mabel, be sure to write me," said Nan, bidding her friend good-bye. "And you, too, Mildred."

"Come down next year," insisted Dorothy.

"I had such a lovely time," declared Nettie.

The locomotive whistle tooted in the distance, calling all the stragglers.

"Good-bye, Aunt Sarah!" called the twins, as the bus moved off. "Good-bye, Uncle Daniel! Good-bye, Harry!"

When the twins and the others reached home, Dinah said a message of great importance had come from Mr. Bobbsey.

"Oh, what is it?" they cried out together.

"I don't rightly know," Dinah replied, " 'cause the telephone connection was bad. But I think it was about the *Sea Hawk.*"

"Oh!" exclaimed Connie. "I—I hope it's good news!"

Dinah was sorry she could give no better information. Mrs. Bobbsey at once telephoned Lakeport. This time the connection was good and she kept saying, "Oh, that's splendid news! Yes, I'll tell her!"

Finally Mrs. Bobbsey finished the conversation, and turned to tell the others the good news. Through his friend in a shipping company, Mr. Bobbsey had learned that at last the *Sea Hawk* was on its way home. Because of an accident to the ship's radio, it had not been possible for it to send messages.

A new appeal had been sent out to other ships

to look for the lost *Sea Hawk*. One had spotted it coming up the Atlantic coast.

"The good news is," said Mrs. Bobbsey, "that the *Sea Hawk* will dock at a port not far from here day after tomorrow!"

Connie was beside herself with delight. "Oh, it's wonderful!" she said over and over. Then suddenly her expression changed to one of fright. "But maybe Father isn't on it!" she said. "Did Mr. Bobbsey say anything about the people on board?"

Mrs. Bobbsey shook her head. "No, he didn't," she said. "But since there was no mention of your father not being aboard, we must assume he is still on the *Sea Hawk*."

The Minturns also tried to make Connie feel hopeful, and at last she smiled again. Surely if anything had happened to her father, they would have heard about it.

"When the *Sea Hawk* docks," said Connie, "please may I go to see it?"

Uncle William said he would take Connie himself. At once the other children clamored to go, too, and it was hard for them all to wait another whole day before finding out whether Mr. McLaughlin were aboard.

To keep their minds occupied, Mrs. Minturn suggested a trip the following afternoon to an amusement park a few miles down the coast.

Freddie was so excited that he did six somersaults in a row, and Flossie jumped up and down so many times that her mother said she would be exhausted before they even got started. Hal Bingham was invited to go along, and his mother drove their car.

At the amusement park there were so many things to do that they hardly knew which bit of fun to take in first.

"Let's go to the Underground City," Aunt Emily said.

"What's the Underground City?" Freddie wanted to know.

Aunt Emily explained that a series of canals ran under a little make-believe hillside. They were like streets, and along the curbs were all sorts of buildings.

"Do people live there?" asked Flossie.

"Suppose you wait and see," her aunt smiled.

A few minutes later they reached the Underground City, and Mrs. Bobbsey bought tickets for all the children. There were boats for two passengers, one seat behind the other.

Dorothy offered to go with Flossie so that Nan might ride with Connie. Hal decided he would like to go in a boat by himself. Bert and Freddie were the last in line.

"I want to sit in the back," said Freddie, stepping in, and his mother let him have his way.

Hal disappeared first under the hillside. Thirty seconds later the attendant started Dorothy and Flossie on their way. Nan and Connie were next in line.

"Why do we have to wait so long?" Freddie asked the man.

"So the boats won't bump," he replied. "Now take it easy. And remember, little fellow, keep your arms inside the boat."

"I'll be very good," Freddie promised, and he really intended to be.

A few seconds after they entered the tunnel, the little boy exclaimed in glee. Lighted up on the side was a toy service station with several cars. One was having fuel put into the tank; another was having a wheel put on. Two attendants the size of dolls were doing this work.

"Oh, I want to see them longer!" cried Freddie, as the boat slid along past the exhibit.

"Here comes another," said Bert a moment later.

On their left, well lighted, was a school in miniature. A bell was ringing, and children were hurrying into the building. How lifelike they looked! But they were only about a foot high.

"Oh, please, Bert, can't we go around twice?" Freddie pleaded.

"I don't think so," his brother answered. "We won't have time."

The little boy was entranced by each exhibit as they came to it. On one side of the tunnel was a row of stores with people busy buying dresses and shoes and coats. On the other side were a grocery store, a restaurant, and a candy shop, with a big cane hanging in the window.

"Oh, I wish I could have some of that candy," said Freddie.

"It's probably not real," said Bert.

Suddenly the boys found themselves in total darkness. They wondered if the lights in the tunnel had gone out, or whether this was part of the ride. Freddie was a bit scared, but Bert reached back and patted his knee.

"We'll soon be out of this, I am sure," he said.

Up ahead he heard giggling, and knew that the girls were having a good time.

"I see a light," said Bert presently.

When they came to the next exhibit, Freddie gasped. It was longer than the others, and how exciting!

A miniature house was on fire. Water was being sprayed on it from a chemical truck. A ladder had been set up against the house, and two firemen were climbing it.

All too soon, the boat went past the wonderful exhibit. Near the end of the tunnel was a hotel, with porters carrying guests' bags inside. Then out into the sunshine glided the boat.

Mrs. Bobbsey and the other mothers were waiting for the children. Hal and the girls already were standing on the platform. As Bert's boat came into sight, the attendant caught hold of it.

"Where's Freddie?" cried Mrs. Bobbsey.

Everyone looked. The back seat was empty!

CHAPTER XIX

THE BIG STORM

BERT was too astounded to say anything. He began to tremble in fright. If anything had happened to Freddie, he was responsible!

"Where—what—oh, Bert, where is he?" Mrs. Bobbsey cried out.

Her outburst brought Bert to his senses. The last time Freddie had spoken to him was at the exhibit of the burning building, he said.

"Maybe he jumped out to look at it," suggested Mrs. Bingham, knowing Freddie's fondness for fire engines.

"Oh, if you're only right!" said Nan, and to herself added, "I hope he didn't fall into the water." She asked the attendant how deep the water was.

"Only a couple of feet," the man answered. "I'll go look for your little boy. Kids sometimes try tricks in the Underground City."

He jumped into the boat with Bert, and soon they were going back into the tunnel. Bert held his breath when they came to the burning-house exhibit. Then he laughed in relief.

There stood Freddie inside the exhibit, examining the fire apparatus as calmly as if he had been in a firehouse at Lakeport. He did not even hear the approaching boat, and when Bert said, "Hi there!" he jumped.

The attendant grasped a hook in the wall and held on so the boat could not glide past. Bert helped Freddie aboard, then the man let go.

"Wasn't that make-believe fire the realest one you ever saw?" the little boy asked, just as if nothing had happened.

"Listen, little boy," said the attendant, "if you belonged to me, I'd spank you!"

"Mother's terribly worried, and everybody else," said Bert disgustedly. "Why'd you have to do that?"

"I'm sorry," said Freddie. "When I saw the house burning, I just had to get out and help. I—I forgot it was make-believe."

When the boat came out of the tunnel, the waiting group sighed in relief. Mrs. Bobbsey accepted Freddie's explanation, after he put his arms around her neck and said:

"I'm terribly sorry, Mommy."

A surprise awaited the Bobbseys when they arrived home. Their father had just come!

"Daddy! Daddy!" screamed the younger twins, and tried to tell him a hundred things at once.

Mr. Bobbsey, in turn, said he had good news. When the older twins asked what it was, he merely winked at them. Whatever the news was, he kept it a secret, but puzzled them by his remarks to Mrs. Bobbsey.

"I had hard work persuading her to come," he said, without mentioning any names, "but I finally prevailed upon her."

"Poor woman, I am sure it will do her good," remarked Mrs. Bobbsey. "Emily, I'm afraid that your house has been a regular hotel this summer."

"That's what we like," she replied. "We would not have so much pleasure, I am sure, if our friends were not around us. Did you hear anything more about the lost vessel, Dick?" Aunt Emily added.

"Yes, I made some inquiries. Just before noontime a radio message was picked up with the call letters of the *Sea Hawk*. Evidently they were able to repair their radio, but the message was very faint."

"Do you think they can be near here now?" asked Mrs. Bobbsey.

"The radio failed before it could give the ship's position," he answered. "Of course, it's not due until tomorrow."

An hour later Mr. Bobbsey called Dorothy into the house and whispered something to her. She laughed happily and ran to get the donkey cart.

"I'm going to the station to meet someone, Connie," she said. "Want to come along?"

"What! More company?" exclaimed Connie. "You'll need a larger house soon. I'd like to go, if you'll have enough room."

"Plenty of room," replied Dorothy. "We're the only ones going."

The two girls did not have long to wait at the station, for the train pulled in just as they reached the platform. Dorothy looked about a little uneasily.

"I'm looking for a lady I don't know," she said to Connie. "I hope she's here!"

All of a sudden Connie let out a scream. "Mother!" she cried, running down the platform. "Mother, what are you doing here?" The little girl flung herself into her mother's outstretched arms.

"The Minturns invited me, darling," her

mother answered. "Mr. Bobbsey brought the message. I'm going to spend the night."

"Oh," said Connie. "That was the big secret. Oh, Mother, I'm so glad to see you! And when Father comes tomorrow, we'll meet him!"

Mrs. McLaughlin's face clouded over a moment. Then she decided not to show her anxiety in front of her daughter, and smilingly said, "Yes." She was introduced to Dorothy, and they set off at once.

"You surely had a good rest," declared Connie's mother, "for you have roses back in your cheeks. How well you look!"

"Oh, I've had such a perfectly wonderful time," declared Connie.

"And we'll have more!" exclaimed Dorothy.

At a glance Dorothy saw why Connie was such a lovely girl, for her mother was one of those pretty, fine-featured women, although just now she looked thin and tired.

She smiled happily, however, all the way to the Minturn home, and was made very welcome by the two families. Connie showed her the grounds and the beach. A little later, as they were standing by the water with the others, Bert said:

"I heard we're going to have a big storm."

"Oh, will it be a hurry-up-cane?" asked Freddie.

"Hurricane," corrected Mr. Bobbsey. "I hope we won't have as big a blow as that."

"We had one year before last. It was awful," said Dorothy. "The ocean tried to run over the whole place. It ripped out the fishing pier, and the water came way up to the cliffs."

"I'm sure this one won't be bad," Aunt Emily spoke up quickly.

She had caught a glimpse of Mrs. McLaughlin's face when a storm at sea was mentioned. She knew Connie's mother must be thinking about the *Sea Hawk* and what might happen to it.

Hal came up. By this time the ocean had begun to look very angry. Huge waves thundered in. The horizon became inky black.

"Come on, Bert," said Hal. "Let's go down to the Coast Guard station and see what warnings have been posted."

The boys pushed their way against the wind, which got stronger by the minute. When they reached the station, one of the men, whom everyone called Johnny, came out the door.

"Say, what are you fellows doing here in weather like this?" he asked.

"We came to see what warnings are up," replied Hal.

"Well," said Johnny, "all small craft we could reach by radio have been advised to come in. And, of course, everybody'll have to batten their windows against the storm."

"Do you suppose there are many boats at sea without a radio?" asked Bert.

"The Coast Guard boat," replied Johnny, "has gone out to find them. I think you boys should go home before the rain starts—and that's going to happen any minute."

The boys gladly took his advice and headed for home. They no sooner got indoors when a torrent came down.

"Ooh," said Flossie, looking out the window, "it looks like night in the daytime."

Later, after supper, the children felt a little uneasy with the wind and rain lashing outside. Even the adults were bothered by the severity of the storm. It was suggested that the small twins retire. The others followed after a while.

Many hours later, when all was quiet in the Minturn house, a terrific banging was heard on the front door. Mr. Bobbsey and Uncle William dashed downstairs, followed by all the others except Flossie and Freddie. Mr. Minturn flung open the front door and there stood a big coast guard.

"Sorry to wake you, Mr. Minturn," he said, "but our telephones are out at the station. Do you mind if I use yours, sir? I'm trying to get some other men to help us."

"Go right ahead," offered Uncle William. "I hope it's working."

The telephone was working, and the guardsman put through his call. After he had finished talking, Mr. Bobbsey asked him what was wrong.

"We've had an SOS from a freighter offshore," answered the coast guard. "It's in trouble and is trying to get near the inlet. Our boat is out searching for it now to guide it in."

"What freighter is it?" asked Mr. Bobbsey.

"It's one that's limping in from the south," answered the guard. "Her name's the *Sea Hawk*."

CHAPTER XX

THE REUNION

"MOTHER, Mother!" cried Connie. "That's Father's ship."

"Yes, dear," replied Mrs. McLaughlin quietly, tears forming in her eyes. "Oh, I pray it will get in safely!"

"Do keep up your courage," said Mrs. Bobbsey, putting an arm around the weeping woman's shoulder. "I have a feeling everything will be all right."

Mr. Bobbsey and Uncle William, after donning raincoats, went along with the coast guard.

After they had stepped out into the howling storm, Bert said, "Mother, may I go with them, too?"

"I *must* go, Mother," Connie said bravely. "I want to help save Father."

Nan and Dorothy spoke up quickly. They also wanted to join the others on the beach. The three mothers agreed to let the children go, provided they stayed together.

"We'll be along later," Mrs. Bobbsey said, "after I tell Dinah to keep an eye on Freddie and Flossie."

The four children put on their rubbers, raincoats, and rain hats and, holding hands to battle the strong winds, set off for the beach.

They ran as best they could along the sand to the inlet. But they could not find Mr. Bobbsey or Uncle William.

"What are those red lights?" asked Nan, as two big red flares burned vividly on the rocks at the entrance to the inlet.

"Signal lights," answered Bert. "They use them because they cut through the black night better. It's hard to see through this driving rain."

"Oh, I hope the *Sea Hawk* will see them!" cried Connie.

"So do I," answered Bert. "Where do you suppose Dad and Uncle William are?"

There were a number of men going back and forth on the rocks, carrying ropes and lifebelts. They all looked alike in their raincoats and sou'-westers.

"Bert, isn't that Hal Bingham?" asked Nan.

"Yes." Bert shouted, "Hal—Hal—over here!"

When Hal joined them, they worked their way

over to a group of men trying to rig up a searchlight. The men were having a struggle against
the wind and rain.

"She'll blow herself out yet," yelled one of the
men. "This storm can't last much longer."

"There's Dad!" shouted Bert, pointing to one
of the men who were struggling with the portable
searchlight.

"Dad," asked Nan, "is there anything we can
do to help?"

"No," answered Mr. Bobbsey. "Not right
now."

"The Coast Guard cutter is coming in!" Uncle William shouted above the noise of the storm.
"She's coming in alone!"

A silent group stared intently out to sea. The
outline of the Coast Guard cutter could barely
be distinguished as she fought her way into the
inlet.

"Do you suppose the cutter didn't find the *Sea
Hawk?*" Connie said heartbrokenly.

"I'll go back to where they'll moor," offered
Mr. Bingham, who had just joined the group.
"Maybe I can get some information."

At that moment a strange thing happened. A
yellow-gray flash of lightning brightened the
sky, and there, just a little to the left of the inlet,
stood a big vessel. Not a light could be seen on it.

"Look!" everybody shouted at once. "It's the freighter! It's the *Sea Hawk!*"

"She must be on a sand bar," said one of the men.

"I hope so," Mr. Minturn shouted. "As long as she stays on the sand bar, there's a chance of saving her. But if she's blown off, she'll break to pieces on the rocks."

The thought of her father being dashed against the wild rocks made Connie bury her face against Nan's shoulder. Nan could feel her sobbing.

"Oh, the *Sea Hawk* mustn't blow off the sand bar!" she cried. "It mustn't!"

A few seconds later the Coast Guard got the big searchlight into operation, almost turning the black night into daylight with the blinding white glare. Soon the beam was shining directly on the *Sea Hawk,* which was being washed by towering waves.

The people on shore could see men leaning against the rail of the *Sea Hawk*. Their faces were not clear, but those on shore could see them waving their arms wildly. How glad they must have been to spy rescuers!

The sea was so wild it was impossible to use the lifeboats to come ashore, so the guards were making a breeches buoy ready.

"They're going to shoot the line out now!" shouted Hal.

At that very moment there shot out to sea a harpoonlike gadget carrying a thin rope.

"They've got it on the ship!" exclaimed Mr. Bobbsey. The line was attached to a heavy cable, which the men on the ship started pulling in.

"What happens next?" asked Bert. He had never seen a breeches buoy in action before.

"Well," said his father, "they fasten the end of the cable high up on the ship."

"Oh, I see," said Bert. "The line will stretch tight and the breeches buoy can run on a pully from the ship to the shore."

"Right."

"There goes the breeches buoy!" cried Hal. The odd-looking buoy swung out over the waves. It was like a life preserver with short canvas breeches attached.

The wind had died down a little and more people had come to watch the rescue. Among them were the twins' mother, Aunt Emily, and Mrs. McLaughlin. When they saw the children, they hurried over.

"Has anyone heard if my husband is on board?" asked Mrs. McLaughlin excitedly.

Mr. Bobbsey, who came up to the group, told her that they would soon know.

"Here it comes! Here it comes!" called the crowd as the breeches buoy neared shore.

Up and down among the waves it bobbed, sometimes seeming to go all the way under. Closer and closer it came.

Everyone stood still, watching breathlessly. Connie clung close to her mother.

"He made it!" shouted Bert, as the man in the buoy reached shore.

The poor fellow was nearly exhausted when the men reached him, but he insisted on walking up instead of being carried. Beneath his heavy woolen jacket one arm was in a sling.

Everybody gathered around, and Connie, unable to control her anxiety any longer, broke through the crowd to see the rescued man.

"Oh—it—is—my father!" she screamed, running toward the bewildered man. "Father! Father!"

"Connie! My little Connie!"

The bewildered man blinked as if he could not believe what he saw. Then, with his good arm, he held her tight.

Mrs. McLaughlin ran up to them, looking on speechless, almost too overcome to trust that what she saw was true.

"Clara!" he cried.

Mr. McLaughlin drew his wife close to him,

and not a word was spoken for several seconds. Then she introduced the Bobbseys and Minturns, and Aunt Emily suggested that they take the rescued man up to the house at once.

Mr. Bingham and Hal, who had been anxiously watching the reunion, stepped up to Mr. McLaughlin. "Is George Bingham out there?" Hal's father asked.

"Yes," came the answer. "Captain Bingham is safe."

While Hal and his father stayed to watch the rescue of the captain and his crew, the others went with Connie's father to the Minturn house. Dinah was awake, and quickly prepared hot coffee for him.

Mr. McLaughlin was given dry clothes. He changed quickly, then while he ate some food and drank the coffee, he told of his strange voyage. Connie and Mrs. McLaughlin sat on either side of him and listened eagerly, as well as the Bobbseys and the Minturns.

"Well," began the rescued man, "from the very beginning of our voyage we had trouble. Storms, water shortage—

"When we arrived in the East Indies, our teakwood was not ready and we lost time there. I wrote a letter home but apparently it never arrived. And just to make doubly sure my wife and

Connie wouldn't worry, I had my cabin boy send a cablegram—"

"It went to the wrong address!" Mrs. McLaughlin exclaimed.

"Did you run into much bad weather on the way back?" asked Mr. Bobbsey.

"We were about a hundred miles out in the Indian Ocean, when the first storm hit us," Mr. McLaughlin said. "Then our troubles really began. First, our rudder broke. Then, to add to that, our radio wouldn't function. We drifted miles off our course."

"All bad things seem to come at once," sighed Mrs. Bobbsey.

"How true!" replied Connie's father. "Our next worry was the cargo—it shifted in the storm, and all the crew who weren't working on repairs had to move lumber.

"That's when I broke my arm, and it hasn't been right since, but now I'll have it set properly. Finally we solved the problem of the lumber and luckily the storm passed."

"Then everything was all right?" asked Nan eagerly.

"Not quite," Mr. McLaughlin said. "We put in at one of the uninhabited islands for fresh water and tried to make repairs to our rudder and radio. Our extra radio parts were smashed in the storm, so poor Sparks, our operator, tried to rig up an emergency set."

"Were you on the island long?" asked Bert, completely enthralled by the story.

"Yes," replied the officer. "Longer than I expected. We were on the island only a few days when several of the men became sick. They ran a high fever and we were afraid to put to sea, not knowing the nature of the illness."

"What happened next?" asked Dorothy excitedly.

"Well, after the men recovered, we set out again. Our radio still wasn't working, but the operator kept trying. We were finally on our way home when we ran into the hurricane. Then suddenly our rudder started acting up again.

"Luckily Sparks had the radio working by that time, and we were able to get an SOS through. We limped along and then ran aground, and—well, here we are!"

"Whew!" said Bert. "What a story!"

Just as Mr. McLaughlin finished, there was a knock on the door. Hal and his father came in with Captain Bingham, who was introduced.

The captain said that all the officers and crew had been taken off the ship, and that the *Sea Hawk* was no longer in danger of smashing up on the rocks, since the storm was subsiding.

"Matter of fact," Captain Bingham went on, "we'll probably pull her off the sand bar at high tide tomorrow. We'll get in touch with a couple of tugboat captains to do the job."

"Fine!" Mr. McLaughlin exclaimed. "The cargo is safe, and the treasure, too!"

Everybody looked at Connie's father in surprise.

"Treasure?" Bert cried out.

"We'll all board the *Sea Hawk* tomorrow, and I'll show it to you," said Captain Bingham with a wink. "Until then, it's a secret."

CHAPTER XXI

A PIRATE'S SECRET

"MY, what a busy day we have ahead of us!" said Mrs. Bobbsey at breakfast. "I wish I might go in the launch with you children to watch the tugboats pull the *Sea Hawk* from the sand bar. But I must pack our clothes, and buy some things to take home from the seashore."

"Are we really going home?" asked Flossie, who did not want to leave the seashore.

"And I haven't found my sea serpent," said Freddie. "Why can't we stay longer?"

His mother said that she thought Aunt Emily had been very kind to have them as guests as long as she had, and also that school would be starting in a little while. They must go home and get ready.

"Oh dear!" sighed Flossie. "I wish I could be two little girls. Then one of me could stay at the seashore, and the other could go to school. I love school!"

Mrs. Bobbsey warned the small twins that they must be very good during their ride on the launch. With a twinkle in her eye, she added that they might even be able to have a trip on the *Sea Hawk* itself. She had heard that Captain Bingham was going to take his freighter with the load of teakwood into the near-by port as soon as the vessel was floated.

Freddie was so excited that he ran around the house making queer sounds like some wild animal, and even leapfrogging the seats of two dining-room chairs. His Aunt Emily warned him that he had better take care he did not have a bad spill and spoil his chances of going on the trip and of coming to her party.

"Party?" asked Freddie, standing still.

Aunt Emily smiled. "Since you must leave tomorrow, I am planning a party supper."

Freddie wanted to know if there were going to be prizes and everything, like a real party. Nan, who had just come in and heard his remark, said, "Sh! Freddie, you shouldn't ask such things."

But his aunt did not seem to mind and said he should wait and see. The next moment Mr. Bobbsey came in and called:

"Everybody ready?"

The Bobbsey twins, Dorothy, Connie, and

Hal came from various directions, and they walked with Mr. Bobbsey and Mr. Minturn to the inlet. There the launch they had hired was waiting for them. The excited children ran aboard, and in a few minutes Captain Brown, who was in charge, gave orders to pull out.

In the distance could be seen the *Sea Hawk,* tipped slightly to one side, and two tugboats which were puffing and chugging. As the launch drew nearer, Freddie began to imitate the sounds of the tugboats. It was almost as exciting as going to a fire, he thought. Bells were clanging, whistles tooting, and there was plenty of smoke floating out over the ocean.

"Daddy," said Freddie presently, "why do they have all those doormats around the tugboats?"

His father laughed, and said the big protective bumpers did look like doormats. He explained that sometimes the tugs nosed right up against other vessels, and the heavy hemp bumpers kept them from causing any damage.

"Are they going to bump the *Sea Hawk* to get her off the sand bar?" Freddie wanted to know.

His father said he did not know. At the moment heavy lines had been stretched from each side of the stern of the *Sea Hawk* to the two tugs. First the tug on the right would steam out, and move the freighter a little in that direction. Next the other tug would pull the freighter in its direction.

"What are they trying to do?" asked Bert.

His father said they were hoping to free the freighter from the sand which was holding it.

"Look! Look!" cried Freddie excitedly a few minutes later. "That tug's going to bump!"

Sure enough, Captain Bingham and the tugboat captains seemed to have decided upon a new method. Now the tug on the right pulled the *Sea Hawk,* while the tug on the left pushed against it as hard as it could.

"I guess that's going to do the trick," said Bert, who was almost as excited as Freddie.

He was right. It suddenly seemed as if all the sand under the freighter had dropped away, because the ship suddenly slid freely into deeper water and righted itself.

"Hurrah! Hurrah!" cried Flossie, and all the others on board shouted in delight also.

"Now may we go aboard?" asked Freddie.

Mr. Bobbsey said it would take some time for the *Sea Hawk* to get its engines working, but the launch could come a little closer. Now that it was safe, they would ask Captain Bingham if he wanted any passengers.

The captain was on deck as the launch came

a few feet away, and he called down to them that the engineer was having a little trouble getting the ship started. In the meantime, they would put a gangplank from the freighter to the launch, and the others could come aboard and see the treasure.

Hal was first to cross from the launch to the *Sea Hawk*. Bert followed, then the older girls, and Mr. Bobbsey and Mr. Minturn brought up the rear, each holding a small twin by the hand.

How exciting it was to be on a freighter that had been halfway around the world and had had such adventures! Captain Bingham took the children on a tour of inspection, showing them where the officers and crew ate and slept. Freddie was very good. Finally he could not wait any longer to find out about the treasure, so he asked where it was and what it was.

"It's in my cabin," replied Captain Bingham, chuckling. "It's a pirate's treasure!"

"Oh!" gasped all the children.

Under the captain's bunk was a locker. He opened it and carefully pulled out a battered old sea chest. When he lifted the lid, his visitors were astounded at what they saw inside.

A heap of gold pieces, strange but beautiful necklaces and rings, and in a smaller box several gleaming jewels!

"When we finally reach land," said Captain Bingham, "this treasure, which we dug up on an abandoned island, will be divided equally among all the men."

Nan looked at Connie. She squeezed the girl's arm and whispered:

"Connie, your family will have plenty of money now. You and your mother will not have to worry any more."

There were tears in Connie's eyes. She did not answer, and after a few minutes said she would like to go and find her father. He was busy working with the men who were trying to start the engines.

When she found him, Connie told her father about how kind everyone had been in giving her money. Now she wanted to give that money to the Fresh Air Camp to help make other unfortunate children happy, just as she herself had been helped.

"And Father," she said, "please may we give something very special to the Bobbseys?"

Her father said he thought this was a good idea, and when they got to the port where the teakwood was to be unloaded, the two of them would go shopping.

This was how it happened that after the engines of the *Sea Hawk* started working, and the exciting trip was made into port, that Connie and her father left the others, saying they would be home later.

At six o'clock everyone was dressed for the party, and Aunt Emily called them to the table. What a pretty sight it was! At each place were little souvenirs to remind the visitors of their visit to Ocean Cliff, and in the center stood a toy freighter. On the deck were several men. But they were not sailors—they were pirates!

Everyone laughed, and the fun kept up through the whole meal. Dinah and the Minturns' maid had worked hard all day to make the meal particularly fine.

Good as the food was, and gay as the party turned out to be, the one thing which pleased the Minturns and Bobbseys more than anything else was the happiness in the faces of the three reunited McLaughlins. Nan thought she had never seen three more joyful people.

At the end of the meal Connie made a little speech. She said she and her family would always be grateful to the others for all that had been done for them, and they wanted each family to have a remembrance.

She handed a package to Mrs. Bobbsey and another to Mrs. Minturn. When they opened them, what lovely surprises! Inside were two beautiful silver tumblers, which might be used for holding flowers, as well as for drinking.

"Oh, how very lovely!" exclaimed Mrs. Bobbsey. "We shall take very good care of these and always treasure them."

"And we want you to come to Iron City and see us," said Mrs. McLaughlin. "Our house is not so large as yours, so we can't have you all come at once, but I do hope you and the Bobbseys will not forget us."

"No chance of that!" said Dorothy. "And I will come to Iron City any time you ask me."

Directly after supper the McLaughlins said good-bye. They were going to stay at a hotel near the *Sea Hawk*.

Next morning there was hustle and bustle in the Minturn house. An expressman came to take the Bobbsey trunk, and a truck came to carry the suitcases to the station. The grownups were to ride to the train in the Minturns' car, but the twins had begged for a last ride in the donkey cart. They would start out ahead of time with Dorothy.

"I don't know how to say good-bye to you," said Dorothy as they set off. Usually she was so full of fun, but now she looked really sad.

"Mother said maybe you can come to our house for Thanksgiving," said Nan.

"Oh, that will be wonderful!" cried Dorothy, and smiled again.

"Just the same, I don't think we'll ever have so much fun again as we had here," spoke up Flossie.

But the little girl did not guess right. If you want to find out how much fun she had during the next winter, just read about Flossie and her brothers and sisters in *"The Bobbsey Twins at School."*

When the donkey cart reached the station, there was Hal Bingham waiting to say good-bye. He and Bert walked off a little to one side and made some private plans about getting together again. Finally the train rolled in and the Bobbseys climbed aboard.

"Oh, if we only didn't have to leave our friends!" said Nan, as she waved a last good-bye to Dorothy.

"I certainly liked Hal Bingham," declared Bert.

"Good-bye, ocean!" cried Flossie as the train made a turn, and took the Bobbsey twins away from the seashore.

"Good-bye, sea serpent," sighed Freddie. "I'll get you next time I come!"

Don't miss **THE BOBBSEY TWINS AT SCHOOL,**
the story of the twins' exciting winter at home
and their hilarious adventures with their school
friends.